Flirting With Temptations

SOME LINES AREN'T
MEANT TO BE CROSSED

Janae Marie

JM Publications

PUBLICATIONS

Flirting with Temptations Copyright © 2012 by JM Publications.

Editor: Jenetha McCutcheon
at www.quilleditorialservices.com

Cover Design: Donna Osborn Clark at
www.CreationByDonna.com

Interior Design and Typesetting by:
www.interiorbookdesigns.com

Janae Marie Contact Info:

E-mail Address: krysrieon@yahoo.com

Blog Address: janaemariepubs1.blogspot.com

ISBN: 978-0-615-67426-1

To my baby girl; Kayla Riley H, you are my true inspiration for doing this. I hope when you grow up, you can look back and be proud. Also, special thanks to my family for wanting nothing but the best for me.

Prologue

S mart, sexy and sophisticated are just a few words to describe Monica Clayton. She is a young successful senior marketing exec at Shears & Perry marketing firm and a single mom to a five year-old little girl. The petite redbone with long, beautiful, brown hair and hazel eyes appears to be just an ordinary hardworking black woman, but she is anything but. Monica Clayton is a vulture and this time she is going to get him.

This time would be different because she is a fighter. Her words of motivation are; "through any means necessary...I shall not accept defeat." Truer words have never been spoken. But you'd think she'd be fighting to survive in this world rather than trying to trap a man. Monica Clayton is the type of female who gets what she wants any way she wants. Her victims of choice are married men. The pursuit of a married man gives Monica an adrenaline rush. There is something sexy about seducing a man to succumb to her every desire. She has had her eye on a rather sexy chocolate co-worker for some odd months. And now is the time to put her plan into action. Men are mere toys to her, to be used for her sexual satisfaction. Men are accepted as players, loving and leaving as many women as they can possess. Why couldn't a woman? A certified man-eater who always keeps a hearty appetite would soon reach her breaking point when she eventually crosses a line that should've never been crossed.

Her Beginnings...

onica is standing in the executive suite office located at the top floor of the building with Senior Chief Executive Jonathan Perry. This time was usually reserved for their noon time quickies before she headed back to her office. A secret affair that only the two of them knew about had gone on for years before things got too heated up between them. The fact that the suite was the only office on the floor and keys were available only to the chief executive was perfect for them. This allowed them to be alone with no witnesses, and no nosy co-workers to go and spread her dirty little secrets all around the office. The person they were hurting the most was; Jonathan's wife Adele. But this little tidbit didn't bother Monica at all as she stood in front of him while he stared out of his office window admiring the scenery.

"Hello Mr. Perry... How are you doing today?" Monica asks flirtatiously.

He turns around in his chair to walk over towards Monica.

"Why hello, Monica, might I say you are looking awfully sexy today? You know you have the sexiest legs on any woman I've seen," Jon says, as he reaches out for a hug from her.

"I missed you today Mr. Perry. Your assistant needs her daily dose of you," Monica answers.

"I know, I know. I missed you today, too," he replies as he places his hands around her soft firm body. He runs his hands along the sides of Monica's hips as he pushes her against the wall. Jon plants several kisses on her neck before he undoes his pants and lifts up her skirt. He then grabs her legs and wraps them around his body and enters her slowly. Tighter and tighter, Monica strongly holds onto Jon as he thrusts vigorously inside. He knows his affair with Monica is wrong and that it has to end at some point. But free and available pussy on the side is hard for any man to turn down. Plus, messing around with Monica relieved a lot of stress and tension that he felt being CEO of the company.

Their casual sexual trysts were sometimes the high-light of Monica's workday. What started off when she was his part-time temp assistant as a college intern with the company turned into a full-time position not only with Shears & Perry marketing, but with her supervisor as well. Her plan was fool-proof; she'd have the corporate job along with a little dick on the side. What could go wrong? She saw no wrong in that.

Monica became overcome with pleasure as her juices flowed like a river cascading down her thighs. Again, he did it right, pleasing her to the fullest extent. This is a job he does exceptionally well many times over. Monica knew she never wanted this moment to end.

"Shit, I have to tell you something, Monica," Jon informed her as he leaned against his desk to button his pants.

"What, what is it?" she questioned, she sat in front of him on the floor with her legs spread wide.

"You know I enjoy being with you. It's been a nice several years but I can't keep doing this Monica. I can't do this anymore," he tells her.

"What the hell do you mean you can't do this anymore? You can't do what anymore? Work with me? Fuck me...what?!"

"Both, actually, Monica, I don't feel too good about this. I never felt good about this."

"You don't feel too good about this...well you weren't thinking about that when you were fucking me. We've been seeing each other since you hired me into this company almost ten years ago," Monica argues, rising to her feet.

"Yes, Monica I know. You are a very qualified marketing exec. That's why I promoted you to that position. I just don't want word to get out about us. Trust

me, that wouldn't do anything for either of our reputations. Besides, I think my wife may be starting to suspect
something and I'd hate for her to find out and try to hurt
you."

"It seems as if you're trying to blow me off," Monica
pouts.

"Don't look at it that way. I'm not just leaving you.
I'm leaving this office and going to work in San Francis-
co. My wife got a job offer and I'd be managing this firm
over there. This is my last day." Jon tries to console as he
reaches for Monica to sit on his lap.

"Look what we had was fun sweetie, but all things
must come to an end. You are a senior marketing exec
now. Focus on that."

"How long did you know that you were leaving?"

"Does it really matter? I'm telling you now," Jon
states.

"How long, Jonathan…?"

"Six weeks…"

"Six weeks! You knew you were leaving a month ago
and didn't tell me? You were just going to keep screwing
with me until you got what it is you wanted, huh?!"
Monica shouts.

"Calm down, it's really not as serious as you are making it out to be Ms. Clayton. You will still have your job
and if you work hard, in a year or two, you too may
become CEO of this firm."

"Oh that's it huh, we're back to formal titles now? It was all good until you got bored because your dick started to get a fucking conscience? Where the hell was that conscience when you had me work long nights just to be bent over your desk taking it up the ass!" Monica yells, as she gets up and walks over to the door.

"MONICA!" he yells as he pounds his fist on the table.

"That is enough! I am still your superior!" Jon walks over to Monica and whispers in her ear a lesson that she could take with her for life.

"You need to realize that in this world when you lie down and open your legs to a married man, he deems you as just that, 'open legs and free pussy.' Get over it. You did it to yourself, Monica. Now, I'd like for you to leave while you still have your job left," Jon says as he opens the door for her. Frustrated and a little embarrassed, Monica gathers her belongings and walks out of the office.

Monica couldn't believe Jonathan had just played her like that. How could he just fuck her over so many years then just toss her to the side as if she is a piece of meat? Although, he did have a point; when you present yourself as a woman who gives it up so easily, you can't expect men to maintain any respect and dignity for you; especially if you have none to give to yourself. Sadly, this incident stayed with Monica and hurt her more than she

thought, sending her on a downward spiral of meaning-
less affairs.

Chapter 1
The Thrill of the Chase

~The Next Couple of Weeks~

Monica is at work sitting with a couple of friends in the cafeteria while they are on their break during lunch. She is twisting her fork into her pasta chicken salad. She sits across the table from her best friend Rachel Moore and two other co-workers. As they are discussing important topics of the day, a male co-worker, Keith Jackson, walks past the ladies.

"Now that man is oh so fine! I mean dark chocolate fine! Ooh!" Monica says excitedly.

"Huh, un-uh, now you know that Keith is married!" Rachel answers.

"Um, is that supposed to stop me?! I've always wanted Keith. Simple little things like a man's marital status don't bother me."

"You know you really are something else!!! You are going to get yourself burned one day messing with all of these married men. You know the dirt you do will somehow catch up to you."

"Rachel, Rachel, Rachel, sweetie will you calm down please?! It's just some clean innocent fun," Monica responded.

"Yeah, until someone gets hurt..." Rachel adds, turning her head.

"Whatever!" Monica says laughing it off as she rises from the table and makes her way over to Keith.

"What in the world is wrong with that girl?!" Tina, another senior marketing exec, asks.

"Girl, she's always been like that since college! She doesn't listen to me at all."

Monica is standing by the copy machine making idle chitchat with Keith who is making photo copies for his next report.

"Oh hey, Monica, you look nice today." Keith says with a grin upon his face.

"Thanks, Keith. See you are getting ready for that Tide Reach ad campaign."

"Yeah, you know you're really good at strategizing and coming up with new plans for the team members. Maybe one day you and I should work together," Keith adds.

"Yes we should, most definitely!" she says flirtatious-ly, while we all know that Monica has other interior motives in mind.

Later that day after the break, the workers return to the board room where their boss Mr. Hall begins a few assignments. Monica walks into the room and takes a seat directly across from Keith. As everyone is reaching out for their assigned project folders, Monica with her blouse unbuttoned leans over in front of him and winks at him. Keith tries not to look impressed but his facial expressions show more than any words could ever express.

"Okay, ladies and gentlemen. We have new clientele looking to work with us. Two very prestigious clothing design companies are merging and they want us to help them come up with a new marketing slogan to promote the new image. This will be huge for us so people don't blow it. I have paired you off with workers that I believe will bring out your best ideas. Now I'm expecting my two senior execs to be on the ball with this. This is why I am teaming you up with the wonderful Ms. Clayton, Keith and uh, Keith." Mr. Hall motions for Keith to stand to the side while he tells him something.

"Monica Clayton is a very respectful exec here. So don't get side tracked by her stunning looks. If you lose this account, it won't look good for neither of your reputations. I'm real serious about this one."

"Alright Mr. Hall, I understand."

"I hope that you do," he says walking away.

Keith didn't pay any mind to a word his boss said. He was more fascinated by working alongside Monica. He tried to contain himself, but he knew that this would be one assignment he wouldn't mind working hard at. Slowly, Monica walked up to Keith.

"So Keith, when do you think we can start working on this project?"

"Why don't we get together sometime this weekend? My wife is going out of town, so I'll be alone; just perfect to get some work done."

"That sounds great to me! I guess I'll see you then," she said in a sexy tone as she walked away. Keith was so blown away by the mere attraction this woman embodied that he didn't even realize that his best friend Bradley was waving his hand in front of his face.

"Keith, Keith, Keith!!!"

"Oh yeah, what is it, Brad?"

"Man, we need to talk!" he said as the two men gathered their belongings and walked out of the boardroom.

"Man, I cannot even begin to tell you how excited I am at the thought of working with Monica. Man she is so fine!"

"Keith, Keith, man don't forget that you are a married man. Rochelle is a good woman. Don't do anything to screw that up because you are thinking with your Johnson and not your brain," Brad said as they walked out the building.

"Man, Brad. I know what I got at home. But it doesn't hurt to just look once in a while. You know Rochelle hasn't exactly been on my best of sides lately."

"Didn't you two just have a baby?"

"Yeah six months ago, there isn't any reason why she couldn't work that off –"

"Man I'm not going to stand here and let you criticize your wife when you've just had a baby. But all I am staying is that all Monica has is a pretty face but she doesn't love you like your wife does. Don't throw away six years of marriage on any woman. I'm telling you, Keith, you will regret it."

"I hear you, Brad. I hear you. I don't plan on doing anything with her. But I will keep it in mind Brad."

"Thank you. Just please do that …for me." Keith gives Brad a quick dap. And the two men part ways to their cars.

Chapter 2
The Next Weekend

K eith drives Monica over to the house so they can get started on their presentation for work. Unfortunately, when the two of them step into the house they are drenched from the terrible rainstorm outside. Monica takes off her soaked coat and tries to dry her hair.

"I hate to get my hair wet! I can't believe it poured so much tonight."

"Yeah, I hate rainstorms, too. Why don't I get you something to change in? I wouldn't want you to catch a cold. I'll see what my wife has clean in her closet. I think you two are about the same size." The two go upstairs and Keith frantically looks for an outfit to give Monica to wear. He stumbles upon his wife's silk blouse and designer pants and hands them over to her.

"Are you sure your wife wouldn't mind me wearing her clothes?"

"Oh, of course not; she is a generous person."

"Oh, I see. You and your wife had a baby. She is adorable! Congratulations!"

"Yeah, thanks. She is about six months old now! She is with my wife out of town. They won't be back for about two weeks or so." Keith goes over to the stereo and cuts on some slow, melodic jazz music.

"Oh Keith, where is the bathroom? I need to change out of these drenched clothes."

"It's right down the hall to the right." Keith knew what he was thinking was not morally right. But he just knew that if he didn't seize the opportunity it would not come again. All the thoughts of Rochelle and the new baby leaped out of Keith's head. He walked over to the mirror and gazed at the reflection he saw, then at his wedding ring then again at his reflection.

Suddenly, he heard Monica's voice ask if he's given any thought about their recent assignment. At that moment of hearing that sweet angelic voice he knew he had to have her.

"Oh no, not as of yet, I haven't!" he yelled out to her. He slipped off his wedding ring and hid it in the back of the drawer underneath some old papers. Monica stepped out of the bathroom looking so breathtaking. He never saw his wife's clothes look quite that good in a long time. At that moment he wished he was married to Monica with her close to Victoria's Secret body instead of Rochelle. Not that there was anything wrong with Rochelle's body. She once embodied the shape of a Coca-Cola, but that was before the birth of the baby. Monica gave Keith what he was lacking at home: intimacy. Ever since the birth of Leona, Rochelle hasn't been quite the same loving and affectionate spouse she used to be, thus leaving Keith feeling ignored and resentful.

Monica searches for her work bag with the notes and assignments given to them from their boss.

"You know, I was just thinking. Why don't we go over these tomorrow? It's so late." she stated, fixing her eyes on a clock that read 4:15 am. "You know I really think I should be getting home."

"No, no! No woman is going to be driving home in a dreadful rainstorm at four in the morning. Why don't you stay over? We can work on the account first thing tomorrow morning over breakfast. How does that sound?"

"Alright, fine, since you are twisting my arm!" she said as she laughed touching Keith's hand.

At that moment, Keith knew letting a moment like this get away would be foolish. He had to have Monica, even if it was just for one night.

"Well, I'll sleep on the couch downstairs."

"What, you don't want to sleep on that hard sofa bed. You can sleep here in the bed with me. You know that's if you don't mind. Nothing will happen. I promise I'll be a good boy," he laughed as he ran his hand across his chin. He stood against the wall seriously hoping that Monica would consider his offer. She walked towards a table, grabbed the remote and plopped on the bed.

"So, it's just one night right? There is nothing going on between us; just two adults sharing a bed."

"Yes, ma'am exactly nothing more nothing less," he says nervously as he sat next to her gazing into her caramel eyes.

"Well, what's on TV then? Why are you staring at me like that?"

"Uh, no reason, no reason at all…"

"Why are you so far away? This is your house right, than you should get comfortable. Take your shoes off. You don't have to be afraid of me, I don't bite. You can come closer to me, if you'd like."

Keith decided to get into the moment. He stripped down to his boxers and wife beater. Monica never took one eye off of Keith as he undressed. Impressed by the muscular build and tone in his body, she knew seducing him would become effortless. She was a woman who got any and everything she wanted. And tonight would be the night that she would have Keith Jackson.

Chapter 3
It's Morning...!

Early the next morning, Monica turned over in the queen-size bed, as the sunshine peaked through the Venetian blinds and greeted her face. She looked around the room, but there was no sign of Keith anywhere. Then she smelled the faint aroma of breakfast being cooked. Rising out of the bed with a smile upon her face, she went downstairs to see Keith cooking breakfast for the both of them.

"Well, rise and shine sleepy head! How are you today lovely?!"

"I'm just great, Keith. Is all this for you?"

"No, for us, I have chocolate chip pancakes, Belgian waffles, bacon, scrambled eggs, toast and two glasses of orange juice. Eat up, I was thinking, after we work on the account I'd take you shopping; how about Neiman Marcus?"

A child-like grin came across Monica's face, as no man has ever offered to take her shopping to spend money on her.

"Oh, and don't worry. Money is no object. Get whatever you like."

"Excuse me-Are you serious?" she asked with a big smile on her face?

"Yes, I am. Eat up; there is plenty of food for the both of us."

Later that day, Monica was like a kid in a candy store. She took Keith up on his word about money being no object. She tried on almost every dress in the store. Keith paid for everything from two pairs of Manolos, some Jimmy Choos, and a lovely pair of Christian Louboutin shoes.

She walked out that store with outfits from Dolce & Gabana, Fendi, and Prada, along with the matching bag. Monica was going to have it all, plus some. Keith was showing her a lifestyle that she had never been exposed to before. This was a life that she could get used to. She wasn't sure if she wanted to make Keith hers and hers alone but she definitely knew that she wanted to take part in the luxurious lifestyle that was being offered to her. She felt like a celebrity walking on red carpet. Nothing or no one was going to take this euphoric feeling away from her. Keith was giving her everything she wanted. She never had a man spoil her rotten before.

After the shopping trip was over, Keith finished the night off with dinner at Andiamo's. Monica knew sponging off some other woman's man was no good, but he didn't mind offering.

"Oh my goodness, it's beautiful in here!"

"You've never been here before? Who wouldn't take a stunning woman like you out to such a lovely restaurant like this?"

"So, I take it you've been here before?" Monica asked, puzzled.

"Yes, several times with my wife. But I've never quite enjoyed it like I've done right now."

"Don't you miss your wife?"

"Why are you concerning yourself with matters that don't apply to you? Now what do you want to order? Get anything you want, sweets! I'm good for it."

"Keith you don't have to do all of this-"

"Sweetie, please don't act like you aren't enjoying this. You're a beautiful, sexy woman who deserves nothing but the best, and I want to be the one to give it to you. After dinner we can work on our assignment. You know we only have two days left. Did you decide on what you wanted?"

"Um, the Fettuccini Alfredo with salmon looks pretty good."

"Then order it. You know...I really like how things are progressing between us." he says, as he grabs her hand to join his. He stares into her eyes and says the one thing that Monica never wanted to hear.

"I may be willing to leave my wife for you."

Monica, sipping her drink, chokes at Keith's outlandish comment.

"Are you serious?"

Before Keith could answer her question, the waiter appears asking if they were ready to order.

Chapter 4
Their Secret Meeting

During the next few days at the office, their boss calls everyone into the board room to see how they were doing on their assignments. During the middle of a presentation given by Mr. Hall, Keith slips Monica a small note that read, "Meet me in the bathroom."

Monica looks up at Keith and smiles as he exits the room. Rachel nudges Monica on the shoulder, but she simply ignores her to follow Keith on his request.

Monica slowly and quietly enters the empty restroom seeking Keith. She speaks his name so softly, a male voice appears out of the air letting her know just where to be.

She makes her way to Keith and locks the door behind her. Monica positions herself in front of Keith. He runs his hand down her thigh then moves it up to her behind.

"Damn, hey sexy!"

"Hey, daddy, how are you feeling?"

"Like I need to have you right now, you know you're rocking that skirt. Every day you make it hard for me to work because I can't take my eyes off you."

"Well, why don't you do something about it then?" she stated with a shy smile.

Keith unbuckled his pants and held her close to him. Monica gasped for air as Keith forcefully entered her, never wanting the moment to end. She couldn't imagine how good her life would be once she got involved with him. Messing around with Keith made her forget all the wrong that she was doing by being with a married man. No one knew what was to take place between them and it was just their dirty little secret. She could end it whenever she wanted. But was Monica getting in way too far over her head?

Before everyone left the office at the end of the workday, Rachel ran into Monica near the break room gathering her belongings. She stepped right in front of her and slammed her locker shut.

"Oh my God Rachel, what is your problem today? You've been bothering me all day."

She pulls Monica by the arm over to a corner in the room to talk privately.

"You know what you're doing isn't right! Messing with a married man will *always* come back to bite you in the ass, girl! Please believe that thing called Karma is coming after you."

"Oh wow, will you give it a rest! That man knows exactly what he is doing? Don't get mad at me because I can pull men from just about anywhere. Look, I'm just giving him something he obviously wasn't getting at home."

"Are you even listening to yourself? Come on Moni, think about what you are doing? Think about his wife and how she would feel?"

"I don't know her. Why should I care about her? Don't give me that look. You know I'm just going to do what I want anyway."

"Alright you do that, and see how that shit comes to bite you in the ass."

Rachel walks away with a couple of co-workers while Monica is standing there at her locker. She gathers her belongings and walks past Keith and his best friend Bradley who are getting ready to punch out.

"Goodbye gentlemen, see you tomorrow."

"Bye, Ms. Clayton. Have a nice evening," Bradley stated.

"Mmm, bye Monica, see you later." Keith said with a grin upon his face.

He watches her walk away until his friend hits him in the chest.

"What, Brad man?"

"Come on; don't tell me, you and Monica? Could you be more obvious? I warned you not to go that route. She's like the office slut around here."

"Shh, don't say that man. She's very classy."

"Yeah, but is she worth losing Rochelle and Leona for? Monica doesn't really want to be with you, Keith. She is an opportunist. She sees you're successful and she's a lonely, single woman. She wants a piece of the action. Just think about what you're doing before you get in too deep and lose everything."

Keith looks at Brad then grabs his jacket and briefcase and walks out the door. He knew what Brad was saying was true, but for some reason he felt himself hooked on Monica. What was it about her that he couldn't leave alone? What about Rochelle, his wife for only six years? Was he falling out of love and into love with Monica? Did Monica feel the same way, or was this all just what it was set out to be, just another ordinary fling?

Chapter 5
Surprise, Surprise!!

Two weeks have gone past since Keith and Monica began working on their project for work. They have successfully landed the Desire Clothing account for the firm and came up with a major marketing tool for the company that appeal to a younger age group. Keith decided to invite Monica over to his home just one last time to celebrate their success at work. Monica, again, couldn't turn down the opportunity to see Keith.

In Keith's living room, Monica, takes off her jacket and throws it on to the couch. She walks over to where he is standing near the patio door, and then begins placing her arms around his chest.

"This is truly a beautiful home you have here. I just love this whole house," she says softly.

"You want to go take a swim in the pool?" Keith questioned.

"Of course, it's a lovely night to go for a swim and bask in our success. Don't you think? Why don't I just get out of these clothes and into something a little bit more appropriate for the occasion?" she stated as she began to strip down to her red La Perla underwear. They stepped into the pool and tested the water for a bit. Monica wrapped her arms around Keith's neck as he stared deeply into her hazel brown eyes.

"You know I never thought in a million years that I would have this much fun with you. I could really see myself with you," Keith admitted.

"It's so funny that you say that. I have really been having fun with you as well, but there can never be anything serious between us. I hope you've realized that," Monica replied.

"But why do you say that, love?" he questioned.

"You have a wife, Keith. As fine and sexy as you are, I just can't…"

"Shh! Stop worrying your pretty little self over mundane things. Let me handle that okay! I keep telling you that it is not that big of a deal. I can certainly fix that situation," Keith cut in as he began to kiss Monica passionately then run his hands down her back. She quickly pulled back and started making her way back to the house.

"What's wrong?" Keith questioned.

"It's getting late, and I have some important things that I need to tend to," Monica replied as she began to get dressed.

"Are you sure? Was it something that I said or did?"

"No, not at all, I just have some things that I need to attend to, that's all," she reassured. Monica grabbed a towel by the lawn chairs to dry her hair while Keith walked into the house.

"Well, I do appreciate the time that I spent with you. I hope things don't have to end," he stated as she entered the kitchen behind him.

"I'm sure we can work something out that will benefit the both of us," Monica stated.

"Uh, yeah…" Keith uttered.

"What's wrong, Keith? You look like you've just seen a ghost?" Monica joked. But there were no ghosts; only Keith's wife Rochelle standing in front of them in the living room.

"Uh, Rochelle, when did you get back, honey?!"

"Don't Rochelle me! Tell me why I come home to my darling husband only to catch him kissing the office slut in our pool! What the hell is that?"

"Uh, sweetie I am not a slut!" Monica chimed in.

"What would you prefer I call you, home wrecker, whore?! You knew damn well that Keith was married before you started messing around. I've met you before at the office party last year. So what the hell do you want me to call you?" Rochelle yelled.

"I have been calling and calling you, Keith. I left like five voicemails informing you that I'd be in town soon. But do you bother to pick up the fucking phone? NO! Oh look, the voicemails haven't even been checked yet!" Rochelle yelled.

"I think it is best that I start to head home. I believe that I've done enough damage already," Monica said sadly.

"Oh honey, you think?" Rochelle asked sarcastically. Monica grabbed her things and quickly walked out of the door. Rochelle began to take actions into her own hands. She slapped Keith across the face as she tossed her wedding ring across the room.

"Monica-wait, no Rochelle, I can explain. Baby please let me explain. I'm so sorry!"

"Yes, you are sorry Keith. It's over!"

"Baby please give me a chance to explain!" Keith pleaded with his angry wife.

"You know I'm just five minutes away from doing a Jill Scott in "Why Did I Get Married," and bust a wine bottle upside your head! You better come correct."

"I...just ...I just felt lonely. She was there for me. I wasn't happy. I don't know... I had a weak moment. I felt like things hadn't been the same since the birth of Leona," Keith tried to explain.

"So you mean to tell me that you are blaming your infidelity on your daughter? Come on Keith, that is some pathetic ass shit and you know it! Yes, my body isn't quite the same as it was. But I sacrificed that for us so we could have a family. And now you aren't thankful for it. Well you know what, since you want to run around with Monica so damn much, go be with her. I don't have time for this cheating shit. We took vows Keith. We took vows in front of God. This is how you want to repay our good Lord by cheating on a woman who doesn't want you."

"What do you mean she doesn't want me?" Keith stated, as he slowly began to get angry.

"Keith, Monica is a slut! The only thing she cares about is sleeping with as many married men as she possibly can without any repercussion. You think you're the only one she has slept with? Come on Keith, be for real here. She's messed around with about five other guys at your job!"

"I am so fucking tired of this shit! This is what I'm talking about. You are always making me feel like I'm not good enough. At least when I'm with Monica, she meets all of my needs. I can't do this anymore. I'm ready to leave," Keith responded.

"LEAVE KEITH, if you believe that Monica can do a better job, then go right ahead. Just be prepared to pay some child support for Leona."

"Whatever, I'm through with this shit," he stated as he threw his wedding band onto the floor while Rochelle went upstairs to the bedroom. Keith knew that he was guilty of infidelity. He was devastated that he truly hurt Rochelle. He had to turn the tables around to make things better. Keith couldn't believe that Brad was right. In one moment he lost his wife and his brand new daughter. Was Monica truly worth all of this? Somehow he still wanted to find out. What would he do now?

Chapter 6
Patching Things Up

A couple of weeks have gone past since things *hit the fan* between Keith and Monica. Keith's life has completely spun out of control. In an instant, Rochelle and Leona were gone out of his life. But Keith wasn't giving up on his family so easily and those lonely nights spent sleeping at hotels just couldn't cut it anymore. He decided to try to talk things over with his wife and pray that she would listen to what he had to say. Rochelle is sitting down at a table in the dining room drinking a cup of coffee and reading the newspaper. She looks up at Keith when she sees him sitting next to her.

"What is it that you want, Keith?" she asks, eyes still glued to the paper.

"Do you have to be so cold, Rochelle?"

"Well, you are the reason why things are the way they are right now."

"Rochelle, can you just hear me out. I just want to talk to you for a minute."

"Keith we have nothing to talk about," Rochelle states, as she gets up from the table and turns away from him.

"We are separated, Keith. Last time I checked, you were screwing another woman!"

"Rochelle, I'm sorry…" Keith apologized.

"Yes, you are! Did you ever stop to think about our daughter?" Rochelle questioned as she looked deeply into Keith's eyes.

"I messed up, Rochelle. But please give me another chance. I can't lose you or Leona. Look, how about we just both calm down. How about we go out to dinner next week, just me and you? Please give me a chance."

"I don't know, Keith."

"If you won't do it for me, let's do it for Leona's sake," he stated to Rochelle, as he reached out for her hand and kissed her softly on the cheek.

"I love you Rochelle," he whispered quietly in her ear. She stared back passionately and smiled.

"I will get my sister, Tami, to babysit Leona. I'll give you a chance to explain yourself over dinner, Keith. But don't expect me to fall so easily. Baby steps Keith, baby steps."

"Hey, I'll take that. As long as it means that we are talking again."

"Yeah, do you want something to eat? I was beginning to cook dinner and since you are here and all…"

"I'd love to stay if you'll let me," Keith says.

Chapter 7
Why You So Obsessed With Me?

Several weeks had passed since she had been with Keith. She couldn't believe the way things fell apart between them, but she wasn't one to wait around for a man to make his way back around. She was at Andiamo's enjoying dinner with a male friend.

"So, Marlin what do you do for a living?" Monica questions.

"I'm a Computer Consultant," Marlin, Monica's date replied.

"Oh wow, what do you do at your job?"

"Well, I write, create and repair computer software. It's really just a lot of time spent in front of a computer screen," he laughs.

"Your job sounds really interesting."

"Well, enough about me, what about yourself? What is it that you do pretty lady?"

"I am a senior marketing exec for a very prestigious company. Have you ever heard of Shears and Perry Marketing?"

"Of course, who hasn't? That's a big name! WOW, I didn't know you worked there."

"Yes, I do. I just landed a big account with Desire clothing for the firm."

"You are just phenomenal, aren't you, Monica?"

"Well, I don't like to brag," she states playfully, as she touches Marlin's hand.

As they are eating and carrying on their conversation, Marlin's cell goes off.

"Oh, I have to answer this," he says.

"Okay, go right ahead. I'm going to run to the little girls' room anyway," Monica, says as she walks to the restroom and Marlin answers his call.

"Yes, Kasha, what's going on?"

"Hey honey, I was just wondering when you were coming home. The kids were wondering where Daddy was. How long are you going to be on your business trip?"

"We talked about this Kasha; I'm trying to bring more money to the home. So why are you complaining?"

"Babe, I'm not complaining, I just miss my husband. I want you to be home."

"I know you do, Kasha. Trust me sweetie, I want to be home with you and the kids just as much as you want me to be. I'll be home tonight, hopefully. But if not tonight, definitely tomorrow, I love you. Kiss the kids for me," Marlin stated to his wife, Kasha Turner.

"I will, don't work too hard, hubby. We all miss and love you. I can't wait to see you," Kasha replies.

"I can't wait either. Smooches, much love, talk to you later, babe!" he said hanging up.

*****

Meanwhile, Monica is exiting the bathroom, but runs into Rochelle who was having dinner with Keith the very same night.

"Oh no, what are the chances that I'd run into you?" Monica asks.

"I don't know. Very likely, since you are probably out with another woman's man," Rochelle fires back.

Monica laughs at her statement. "You are funny. You think you know me so well. But you know you're right," Monica replies sarcastically.

"It is women like you that give us good, Christian, GOD-fearing women a bad name. I swear if I wasn't saved, I'd whip your little skinny ass all over this restaurant," Rochelle responds angrily getting in Monica's face.

"Still bitter, I see. It's not me you should be mad at. Don't get mad at me because your husband found me attractive. Maybe instead of worrying why I slept with your husband, you should ask your husband why he slept with me."

"I ought to kick your ass right here right now but I'm here with my husband right now. Yes, I said *MY* husband. He is mine whether you can accept it or not. You will never be what he wants. You will never be *any* man's wife, being a trifling whore. Oh and trust, Monica, karma is a bitch and you will most certainly get yours," Rochelle threatens.

"Your little threats don't scare me, girl. Obviously, it was something he saw in me that he wasn't getting from you. That's why he came to me," Monica states, walking out of the restroom. She returns to her date without a thought in her head of Keith's whereabouts.

*****

The next week at the end of a very long work day, through the corner of her eyes, Monica catches Keith staring rather hard at her. She thinks nothing of it until she gets home. She pulls up in the parking lot of her Lafayette Condominium and after checking her rearview mirror she notices Keith's car parked a little further down the street. She reaches for her cell phone on the back seat of the car and walks toward her condo. As Monica fumbles through her purse to search for keys while closing the door behind her, Keith pushes the door open.

"Monica, I need to talk to you," Keith said making his way into Monica's home.

"Keith, what the hell are you doing here?"

"I couldn't stop thinking about you since the moment we stop seeing each other. I thought I could just let things go and that the affair would be over. But you are nothing like Rochelle; I need you in my life. Monica, I'm in love with you," Keith confessed.

Monica looks around the room for a weapon just in case the situation became dangerous.

"Keith, you are married. I thought you were trying to work things out with Rochelle. I told you that things couldn't work out between us. Now, you need to go. You are going to wake up my daughter. Wait a minute, you were following me, weren't you? You followed me while I went to pick up Ashleigh from preschool. What the hell is wrong with you, Keith?"

"I needed to talk to you. I knew work wasn't the place. I had to express my feelings for you."

"Keith I think you may need to go home. What we had was fun, but it can't go on anymore. Besides, I'm seeing someone new."

"What do you mean you are seeing someone new? You just forgot all about me huh. Just pushed me to the side like I'm some damn piece of meat?" Keith takes a few steps closer to Monica as she steps back.

"Keith, you really need to leave. Have you been drinking?" Monica asks.

"I'm not leaving. I told you that I want to be with you. I'm not leaving until you say you want to be with me, too."

"Oh my goodness…" Monica says under her breath.

"I can't do this, Keith."

"WHY NOT…?" Keith yells, punching a hole in the wall.

"Because you are married, Keith, now will you please keep it down. You are going to wake up Ashleigh."

"Oh, your daughter, I want to see her," Keith says as he walks towards the bedrooms.

"Keith *please* get the hell out of my house! I'm going to call the police."

"No!" Keith turns to Monica and drops down to his knees and hugs her waist.

"I need you. I can't live without you. I want to build my life with you," Keith pleaded with Monica.

"What about your wife, Rochelle?" Monica questioned.

"Why are you worried about her? It's you that I want. I really enjoyed the past few weeks that we spent together," he confessed as he stood up and stared into her eyes while pinning her up against the wall.

"I love you, Monica. I know that you love me too. I won't let our love die. I'll be back as soon as I get things together. I need you, Monica," Keith kisses Monica on the lips before he turns and leaves.

Monica couldn't believe how crazy Keith had turned out to be. It seems like her sweetest fantasy turned out to be her biggest nightmare. How would she show her face at work now? Would Keith hurt her at work? Would she need a restraining order? Things were getting crazy in her life. What about Marlin? How would things be affected between them? Would things turn crazy between her and Marlin if Kasha found out? She couldn't deal with the madness of all this senseless drama. Something had to be done. But little did she know it was just a little too late to turn things around for the best.

Chapter 8
That Thing Called...
Karma

I t's another ordinary day at work--just like any other day. The coffee is brewing and sounds of the copy machine are humming as people tend to their daily assignments. The office gossip was in full effect by the water cooler. Yes, just another day of research and conference board meetings with a new company that is interested in their product being marketed by Shears & Perry Marketing. A day of promoting, selling and project management was a regular day at the office on this Monday morning, discussing how they could better their quota of products sold worldwide when Monica's assistant, Stacy, interrupted the meeting.

"I'm sorry Ms. Clayton, but there is someone waiting to see you in your office."

"Well, did you tell them I am in a meeting...a very important meeting?!" Monica asks as she looks over at Stacy with a frustrated, yet embarrassed look upon her face.

"They said it was very important," Stacy pressed on.

"Well, who is it then?"

"I think it's better if you just go..."

"Okay, okay fine, I'll go. I'm so sorry Mr. Keshena. I will be right back. Again, I surely do apologize. We are just so busy around here lately. Please take a look at the marketing plan that I laid out for you all while I go tend to this brief interruption. I will be right back." Monica reassures, as she walks out of the board room down to her office.

"This seriously couldn't wait until the meeting was over Stacy? You know I'm trying to get that promotion."

"I'm so sorry Ms. Clayton," Stacy apologized as she went back to her desk to answer a business call.

Once Monica stepped into her office, she noticed someone sitting in her chair staring out of the window. She knew there weren't any meetings scheduled for her today, except DresX software. So she wondered who it could be sitting in her office.

"Yes, may I help you?!" she called out to the anonymous figure.

As the chair spun around, Monica went in a state of shock. It was indeed Keith sitting in her chair.

"Keith, what are you doing in my office? I thought you had the day off today?"

"Oh I did. I just couldn't go another day without you. How are you today, Monica?"

"Keith, I thought we talked about this, it's over. We had some fun, but now it's time to move on. And if you excuse me, I have very important clients waiting on me," she explained, as she turned to exit the room.

Keith jumped up out of the seat and ran for the door and locked it with his hand pressed firmly against the glass.

"You are not going anywhere!"

"Keith, what the hell are you talking about? Let me go. I'm in the middle of a meeting," she pleaded.

"NO! I might have lost my entire family because of what we did together. And if you think for a moment that I'm going to let you go without getting something out of this, you are rudely mistaken. I loved you Monica and look what pain you caused me!"

"What the hell do you want from me? There is nothing that I can do. You knew what the risk would be when you started the affair, and now that things aren't going the way you want them to, you want to threaten me?! Keith, leave me alone! Excuse me," Monica reached for the doorknob to leave but, Keith grabbed her arm and pulled her to the floor.

"Now you listen up. I spent a lot of money on you. I have done things that I normally wouldn't do. I may be on the verge of a divorce because of you. If I have to lose everything that I worked so hard to get, then I damn sure am bringing you with me. You are going to pay for this shit! Did you think you could just sleep with me and that'd be the end of it? Did you think you could just break up my family and you could just walk away from everything? Oh no, I'm going to get my end of this little deal, too. You just watch and see," Keith threatens Monica.

Monica just stared at Keith for a moment before collecting herself together and exiting the room to go back to her board meeting. She couldn't believe what had just happened. How could an innocent fling turn so serious? Who ever knew Keith had a psychotic side? Monica didn't know whether Keith was just trying to scare her or, if he really meant what he said. But not wanting to take that chance, she would have to seriously watch herself at work for now on.

Later that day, still a little shook up by Keith's threats Monica made her way to her best friend Rachel's office. A little startled and on edge, Monica shakily closed the door behind her and sat down in front of Rachel.

"What's wrong? You look as if you are going to cry? You didn't land that DresX account?"

"Oh no, it's not that. Of course I landed that account. It's something else. So remember how you have been telling me messing with Keith was a not a good move?

Well, now I think you were right. I'm so sorry that I didn't listen to you," Monica says apologetically

"Oh lord, what happened?" Rachel asks nonchalantly.

"You fell in love with him or something?"

"Of course not, I've always been one to keep my heart out of harm's way. It's becoming the other way around. He threatened me in my own office today. I think he's going to start stalking me or something. I mean what the hell is wrong with these dudes out here today? I don't know how I'm going to work with him."

Rachel takes a look at Monica and rolls her eyes.

"I tried to warn you about messing with Keith but you swore you knew what you were doing. Now you are paying the price for the dirt you did. I mean, what thrill do you get out of sleeping with so many married men anyway? Don't you believe in the "boomerang effect"?"

"The "boomerang effect" girl what are you talking about?" Monica laughed.

"What you put out there comes back to you? You know that thing called, "KARMA!!!" Rachel explains.

"I'm not saying you completely deserve the way Keith is treating you, but you can't be surprised by it. You said yourself that he was really into you. Did you think he was playing the game just like you were? Guys have feelings, too, Monica, and you can't continue to toy with them. Someone is going to end up getting hurt and sad to say it sister, but that person might end up being you!"

"You're right...I should probably break things off with Marlin," Monica says quietly.

"There's another one! Please tell me he's not married?" Rachel questions disappointedly.

Monica stares at the floor and shakes her head. "His wife's name is Kasha. He has two kids."

"Oh Monica, this cycle of yours has to end sweetie!"

"You are so right, I think I need help!" Monica lets out a tear from her eye. She glimpses down at her watch and notices that it's three-thirty. It was time to pick Ashleigh up from pre-school.

"Rachel, it's time for me to pick up Ashleigh. Can you walk me to my car? I don't feel safe. I don't know if Keith is still here."

"Sure." Rachel and Monica exit the room and head for the parking lot. Monica does a lot of thinking about what Rachel says and believes it may be time for her to get her act together. Luckily, she doesn't see Keith's car parked in the lot so she assumes he has left.

"I think I'll be fine, Rachel. I don't see Keith's car in the parking lot. I think I'm safe."

"Alright, Monica, call me if you need me girl!" Rachel states as she parts ways to get into her own vehicle.

Monica starts her car and drives over to the Morris Child Development Center on the other side of town where Ashleigh attends weekly preschool. She pulls up to the parking lot with just enough time to get Ashleigh, but when she enters the building she gets the biggest shock of her life. Monica slowly approaches Mrs. Lee, her daughter's teacher, with a slight worried look upon her face when she doesn't see Ashleigh anywhere in her classroom. As all the other children are getting ready to leave with their parents, Ashleigh is nowhere to be found.

"Mrs. Lee, where is Ashleigh? I don't see her. Did she run to the bathroom?" Monica questions.

"Um, Ms. Clayton, we've been trying to reach you all day. She was already picked up today. I thought you knew."

"What do you mean she was already picked up? By whom...what time?" Monica asks frantically.

"We assumed he was her father. He said you two were married and that he had to pick Ashleigh up early."

"I'm not married! You let her leave with a complete stranger!" Monica yelled, as she ran out of the school and jumped into her car. She pressed her foot on the gas and searched for her child. The mere thought of her child being out in the world with a stranger drove her crazy. What was going on? Was Ashleigh being hurt, abused? Was she even still alive? A million thoughts ran past her mind as she ran lights and weaved in and out traffic. She was going to have to go to jail because someone was going to have to die tonight. The life of her daughter was at stake here. Who could it be? It couldn't be her father. He hadn't been in the picture since she was in diapers. Why would he want to be back in her life now? But as she reached the interstate she pulled over right before she entered the freeway to calm down. The thought of someone hurting her child drove her crazy. Who would want to harm Ashleigh? Then she remembered what Keith said to her earlier. Oh no, it couldn't be. She started the engine and drove over to Keith's place. He was going to be in a body bag by the end of the night if he touched her daughter. Monica just couldn't believe how crazy Keith turned out to be. How could something so innocent turn out to be so dangerous?

Chapter 9
Sending Messages

After finally reaching Keith's apartment, Monica looked everywhere for them, but they were nowhere to be found. So she pulled out her Blackberry and phoned Rachel. This was the scariest moment of her life.

"Yeah, what's up, Moni?"

"Rachel, he took Ashleigh! He took my baby!"

"Wait a minute, who took her?"

"Who else...? Keith. He took Ashleigh out of school. Now I have to find him. I'm going to...I'm going to lose my mind. I can't breathe. Oh my God, I can't breathe."

"Calm down, calm down, did you call the police? Try calling the police and say she was kidnapped. Go home, and get yourself together. I will meet you there in like ten minutes."

Monica hung up the phone and tried to relax long enough to drive home but it was to no success. Still running lights, a police car turned on its siren to pull her over. But she decided there was no point. They may as well follow her home, because if someone was going to go to jail it most certainly wasn't going to be her. Reaching her home she ignored the officer's demands and walked straight into the house, thus making them follow her inside. But when she saw Ashleigh running into her arms her heart melted. She was so relieved to see her little girl alive and well.

"Oh my goodness, sweetie, Where were you today? Who picked you up from school?" Monica questioned her daughter.

"This man name Keith. He said he was your new friend and that it was okay. He took me to get ice cream," Ashleigh replied.

"Did you say, Keith?" As soon as the words were spoken he walked out of the kitchen and stood in front of Monica. But before Monica could sputter any words out of her mouth, two policemen entered her home.

"Ashleigh, honey, go to your room," she requested to her daughter.

"Miss, we have been following you from about a mile back. Now we are going to have to arrest you for failure to comply with authority, speeding and running several red lights," the officer declared, as he motioned for his handcuffs and grabbed Monica's hands.

"Oh, I'm sorry officer; there has just been a huge misunderstanding here. I'm sure Ms. Clayton was just racing back to see her lovely daughter here. You see, I didn't inform my wife here that I'd be picking our little girl up from school. It must've put her in a complete frenzy. I'm sure that was the reason she was racing back home. We just had a miscommunication, that's all. My deepest and sincerest apologies, officer," Keith elaborated.

Monica turned to look at Keith as if he had lost his mind. Where was he getting this *married* stuff from? Wasn't he *already* married? What was going on inside his head?

"Well, I'll let it go this time but let this be a warning, I don't want to have to see you again, Miss."

"Oh no, I'm sure our paths will never cross again. Thank you officer," Monica replied in a relaxed tone. As the officers left to get into their patrol cars, she turned around and slapped Keith so hard it almost knocked him to the floor.

"What the hell do you think you are doing meddling with my child? How the hell did you know where she was anyway?"

"First, I told you we were going to be together. Secondly, I stole your itinerary from your secretary. Why do you keep denying my love, Monica? After everything we have been through, you can just treat me like this..."

"Treat you like what, Keith?! Ashleigh is not your child. Leona is your child. Rochelle is your wife. Last time I checked you two were still trying to work things out. So why can't you leave me alone?"

Keith paces around her condo in a confused state.

"I don't know why you keep concerning yourself with frivolous things. These things don't concern you. You should only be worried about you and me, Monica. I don't see what you see in Marlin? He really doesn't seem like your type."

"How do you know about Marlin?" Monica puzzled.

"I saw you with him at the restaurant when I was with Rochelle. I just didn't say anything. But I understand we weren't together then, I was trying to patch things up with Rochelle."

"Did you touch Ashleigh?" Monica questioned angrily.

"What? Of course not, I just took her out for some ice cream. I'd never hurt a child. I have one of my own. You need your rest. I'll call you tomorrow," Keith states as he gathers his belongings and walks out the door. Monica just couldn't believe all of the craziness this man has put her through today. She was beginning to regret she ever dealt with Keith in the first place. It was one thing to threaten her but to put her daughter in harm's way was another thing. Something seriously had to be done. Rachel finally came banging on the door all in frenzy as she walked inside.

"I'm so sorry Monica. I would have been earlier but the freeway was backed up for about thirty minutes. Where is Ashleigh? Did you find her? Did you call the police?" Rachel questioned.

"She is in her room. I saw her when I got home. Rachel this man is insane! He stole my itinerary from Stacy and picked my daughter up from school. Ashleigh says he didn't touch her though. But I'm going to have to kill this man. I mean it is one thing to put my life in danger, but when you fuck with my child that's another damn thing," Monica ranted.

"Oh my goodness, I am so sorry. Monica. This is craziness," Rachel says in disbelief.

"He has it in his head that we are married, although he is already married. Oh, lord, why me? What did I get myself into? Rachel, I need a favor. I need you to keep Ashleigh for a couple days. I can't risk him hurting her, touching her, or doing anything I might go to jail for and that's not what Ashleigh needs right now," Monica says.

"Sure, totally anything for Ashleigh."

Monica pulls out her phone and calls the police. Now that Keith was gone and could not harm either her or Ashleigh. She had to report him for kidnapping and domestic violence. This man needed to be up under the jail. Seems like meddling with him was the biggest mistake Monica had ever made in her life.

Chapter 10
The Truth...

Several months have passed since the arrest of Keith Jackson for the kidnapping and domestic dispute that took place with Monica. This incident has in fact made Monica more relaxed. Soon Keith Jackson was going to be an insignificant speck in her mind. As she lies in the bed, she rolls over to see Marlin lying next to her. She knew things would be different this time around. Monica realized very quickly that she was indeed dealing with a different type of gentleman. Marlin was everything she wished she had in a mate. He was tall and sexy with a chocolate complexion and was working on becoming the next Bill Gates. All of which sounded like music to Monica's ears right now. She might've slipped up with Keith, but Monica believed she hit the jack pot with this one. Sadly enough though, Marlin was in fact a married man; a man belonging to another woman. Although widely aware of this, she was solely determined to go after what it is she believed was a real man and Marlin fit the description to a tee.

"I must say, Monica, that you are very radiant in the morning."

"Well, you don't look too bad yourself."

"Would you like to order room service?" Marlin asks while they lay in bed.

"You know I really enjoy being here with you. I appreciate a good woman that is just a good listener and friend who enjoys the simple things in life. I mean with Kasha, she thinks I'm made out of money. She's constantly begging me to keep us living like the Joneses. I tell her I have to work damn hard to keep us afloat. Kasha always wants to be kept in Gucci, Prada, Coach, and Chanel with the Louie Vuitton luggage. Shit wears me out!"

"Well, does she work?" Monica questions as she lies on Marlin's chest.

"Of course not, she is a stay at home mom. We have two little boys. She does a great job as a mom but damn woman. Get a baby-sitter and pick up a damn job application. My goodness,"

"Well, you know you won't have to worry about petty things like that from me. I need no one to support me. I'm a senior marketing exec making very nice money and I'll be getting promoted to Sr. Vice President or CEO soon," Monica boasted as she placed her arms around Marlin.

"You know that's what I'm talking about. I need a woman like you that can provide for her own instead of depending on a man to get it for her. I'm going to have to definitely keep you around," he states as he pulls Monica close to him and begins kissing her and slowly moving his hands to massage her lower back.

Later that evening, Monica decides to meet Rachel for dinner. As the ladies are waiting the arrival of their meals Monica sets in to begin dishing about her previous fling with Marlin. She takes a sip of her wine and smiles at Rachel who is eating salad and bread sticks.

"Girl, let me tell you! This man is so fine! He is making serious bread. Rachel, I'm talking about Bill Gates money. He works as a computer consultant. You know those people make money. Oh, and let me tell you this! He is so good in the bedroom too. He is way better than Keith, he be putting it down. I thought I knew everything there was to know about sex but with him... Whew, he taught me a few things, girl!" Monica informs with a mischievous grin splattered across her face.

"Are you even listening to yourself when you speak, Monica? You are blandly telling me about some frivolous fling you had with some woman's man. Damn didn't you learn your lesson with Keith? I guess not," Rachel states annoyed.

"Oh lord, here we go," Monica replies rolling her eyes.

"Yes, here we go. Ever since I've known you from back in college, you have always been, how should I state this, 'dick-whipped.' You've always found pleasure by sleeping, screwing, and being with a man. I don't know what the hell is wrong with you. I'm surprised you haven't caught an STD yet."

"Excuse me!" Monica yells angrily, "I have always used protection, thank you very much," she whispers.

"I do not find happiness in the arms of a man. The men find happiness with me. At least I can get a man. You know you have always been on this damn 'self-righteous' trip. Like, little old Rachel don't ever do any wrong. I am sure you are no saint. 'Who is without sin, cast the first stone.' I don't see you throwing any stones my way, sinner," Monica blurts out with an attitude as their food arrives.

"Girl, calm down. Thank you, miss. I am your girl, all day every day. I am just looking out for you. I don't want anything happening to you is all. Just please I just ask for Ashleigh's sake that you watch the things that you do. I mean are you even thinking about her? Don't you want to be a good role model and set a good example for her?"

"Oh, of course I do. I just...I just..."Monica answers as she tries to choke back her tears. She knows Rachel is telling her nothing but the truth but there is something that is holding her back from going forward. Monica believes by sleeping with all those married men it takes away the deep rooted pain that she kept so hidden within.

*****

After a few weeks, Monica had forgotten all of what Rachel had talked to her about. She was lying in the bed of the Mandalay Inn with Marlin. Things felt a little different than their regular days together. After a few hours of passionate love-making, Monica wanted more mentally and emotionally. She wanted to know where things were going. She couldn't bear just having a piece of Marlin. He was slowly weighing heavily on her mind. Monica was doing something she'd never thought she would do. She was beginning to catch feelings for Marlin. True, he belonged to another, but she was ready to do whatever it took to make him hers. Monica knew if she could get Keith to leave his family, surely, Marlin would be under the same "Monica Clayton love" spell.

Marlin stood in front of the TV set, which was hanging from the ceiling as he dressed and searched for his cellular phone to turn the power back on. Monica lay back on the bed with her eyes pierced on Marlin. She longed for his masculine body and six pack to be hers. But, unfortunately the truth finally caught up to her as he checked for missed calls on his Blackberry. He turned to look at Monica who was still undressed wearing nothing but the blanket wrapped around her naked body.

"Why are you looking at me like that, Monica? Thought you'd be satisfied, you always seem to be any other time," Marlin states to her.

"I just want to know, Marlin, where are things going with us? I mean I really like you and I know you like this too," Monica questions him.

"I do like you. But what do you mean where are things going? They are going as far as these hotel walls will carry us. Why you ask me something so damn stupid?" Marlin laughs.

"How can you just play me like this?"

"Play you? Let's not start this shit right now, Monica. Be glad you are getting some good dick and be quiet. You're getting what it is you want: a good fuck with benefits, right?"

"I just thought that things would progress to more between us. I thought you were ready to leave Kasha?"

"Leave Kasha, girl you must be smoking? Are you serious? Why in the hell would I leave my wife for a hoe like you?" Marlin laughs as he looks at Monica jokingly.

"Why are you saying this to me Marlin? I deserve better than this. You told me you would leave your wife for me," Monica begins to break down.

"Yeah, I also told you that I love getting head. I see you do that too. I mean are you serious? You deserve better? Girl, please. You are the one on your back in a hotel room with a man who is married to another woman. Now I go back home to a loving family, while I assume you go back to um…nothing. But you deserve better. These chicks are crazy out here," Marlin says as he fastens the belt on his pants walks into the bathroom and closes the door behind him.

Monica lies on the bed and bursts into tears. She looks around for her clothes. How could he turn into such a jerk, she asked herself. She couldn't believe he just played her like that. What was she to do? Well, she wasn't going to just let this go? Monica believes despite Marlin's cruel words that she did in fact deserve better, even if this meant tearing his family upside down. Marlin was going to pay for the pain that he caused in her heart. She was never the type to catch feelings for any man unless he was truly special and worth getting her heart. Marlin had played her and she was ready to get her revenge.

Chapter 11
Little Lost Soul

A week has gone past since that tearful night at the hotel. Still brewing on Marlin's asshole behavior, Monica decides to take matters into her own hands. She decides to show Marlin the mistake he was indeed making. Monica parked about a block or two back from where Marlin lived. She spotted his Lexus in the driveway, so she knew he was home. Once she reached his front door, she banged on the door loudly and screamed out his name until he opened up.

"Marlin, Marlin, Marlin!!!! Open the damn door! You better open up this motherfu- door!" she yelled, creating a scene with the neighbors, as she continued to pound on the door.

"Marlin, Marlin, Marlin!!"

As she yells frantically and bangs crazily, Marlin finally opens the door.

"Monica what the hell are you doing out here? Doing all this damn hollering! You are disturbing my family. I have my two boys in the room. Damn, what do you want?" Marlin asks angrily.

Monica pushes pass Marlin and walks into his house. She was ready to confront his wife about his recent acts of infidelity.

"Where is Kasha? Where the hell is she? Is she here? Is she home? She needs to know all about the dirt you did. I'm about to make all of your skeletons fall out of the damn closet," Monica says running off at the mouth.

"Woman, what the hell are you doing? Shut the hell up. Are you trying to get your ass kicked? Trust that my wife will kick your little yellow ass, Monica."

"Don't be trying to scare me. She needs to know about this shit! Kasha, Kasha where are you? Did you know your husband has been sleeping with me for the past two to three months now? Huh, did you know that mess?"

"What are you doing, Monica?" Marlin asks frustrated.

"I just thought I'd hurt you. You know the way you hurt me. Karma really is a bitch isn't it?"

Monica really began to believe that she was getting the upper hand on this one until she got what she wished. Suddenly, Kasha appeared in their dining room from their patio outside. She had been sipping tea with a close friend. Kasha was a short and tiny, but very tough

Latina woman. She wasn't one to back down from a fight. So Monica might've gotten herself into a little more trouble than she bargained for, especially when Kasha's friend came in with her to see what all the commotion was about. It was indeed Rochelle, Keith's ex-wife. She couldn't believe she had to run into her, again. Could this shit get any worse, she thought?

"Marlin, what the hell is going on here? Who the hell is she? Why the hell is she in our home?" Kasha spits out angrily.

"Oh, let me explain. This is the same tramp that slept with my ex-husband," Rochelle spat out.

"Oh, this is Monica. This piece of trash slept with your man?" Kasha stares at Monica and frowns.

"Why are you here? Wait I want Marlin to explain. Did *you* sleep with her? Be honest, don't you dare lie to me. I will beat the shit out of you where you stand, Marlin T. You know I don't play."

"Yes, Kasha I did. While I said I was on business meetings, which I was, but I messed around with her, along the way," Marlin sadly admitted.

"So not only did you sleep with her man, you slept with mine. WOW, you must love being some type of home wrecking, scandalous whore. I ought to beat yo' ass where you stand, but you better be glad my kids are home. They're saving you right now. Cause if they weren't, your ass would be grass. And I'm not telling any lies. So I think it's best for you to leave right now before I forget where I am. But best believe I will come for that ass. I will come when you least expect it, too. Please trust, this is no open threat. I am damn serious," Kasha threatened Monica as she looked up to her, piercing her soul. Monica just stepped back and turned towards the door. As hurt as Monica was with Marlin she was no fool. She could tell Kasha didn't play when it came to her man. Monica was beginning to rethink her decision of ever seeing Marlin in the first place. He was not worth the trouble that she was going to be getting herself into very soon.

Chapter 12
Kasha & Marlin

~While He Slept~

K asha stared in disbelief at her husband. How could he betray her love and trust? How could he just throw away his family like that? Something had to be done. An explanation is needed for a serious offense like this. Kasha paced around their living room, never taking her eyes off of Marlin. She couldn't believe a man she devoted her life to; so that their family could have everything they needed could disobey her trust like that. What was he thinking she thought?

"You got five minutes to explain yourself," she ordered Marlin.

"I don't know what to say Kasha. I have no excuse for what I did to you and the boys. I know I was wrong," Marlin apologized.

"You're damn right you were wrong. I have done everything to make sure this family has been up kept. I make sure you have clean clothes and hot food before you walk through the door. Plus, I get Chris and Jamal together for school every day. I help them with their homework while your selfish ass is too damn tired and busy with assignments from work to help. But you got the damn nerve to sleep with another damn woman. And now you don't have any words to say. Boy, I tell you. You better sleep with one damn eye open tonight and hope that I don't kill you in your damn sleep," Kasha says walking away.

A couple of days later, while Marlin is getting ready for another long day at work he goes down stairs to see Kasha cooking a rather big breakfast. His first instinct is to think perhaps she has forgotten all about the infidelity incident. But no, couldn't be, not this soon. Next he thought Kasha is trying to poison him. She couldn't be over something so serious so quickly. He entered the kitchen a little on edge as he began to greet his wife who was placing a plate of food in front of him on the table.

"Hey honey, how are you doing this morning? Did you sleep well? I hope so. Please don't work too hard. I hate how you come home grumpy after a long day of work," Kasha states as she kisses him on the forehead and takes a seat in front of him at the table.

"Hey, um, I don't mean to bring this up but are you alright? I mean are you over that little incident a couple of days ago?" Marlin asks.

"Oh that? Of course I'm over that. We can work all that out in counseling. Stop worrying about crazy mess like that. Will you just eat your breakfast before it gets cold? You know how you hate to reheat your food," Kasha answers. Marlin is in straight disbelief at Kasha's coy demeanor. He just knew that she'd be a complete tyrant by now. Marlin played with his food just in case she tried to sneak some poison into it.

"Why aren't you eating, honey?" she asks.

"I'm just not hungry. I'm going to head out for work now. I'll see you when I get home," Marlin says.

"Alright, honey. I'll miss you," Kasha jumps up from the table and gives Marlin a big hug and kiss. She walks him to the door and watches as he pulls off into his Lexus. Once he is completely out of sight, she closes the door, ready to put her plan into action. Marlin knew something just wasn't right with Kasha. He has never known her to act so calm and collected. It was almost frightening. He wishes that he could pinpoint what exactly was going on with her because he knew something just wasn't right.

Chapter 13
Kasha & Marlin

~The...Burning~

Later that evening, Marlin comes home tired and exhausted from a long day of work. He turns the corner down Manhattan Avenue to his home when he notices that there is a huge commotion going on. His first instinct was that something must have happened to Kasha and the boys. But as he approached his home it was an even more serious matter. Marlin, pulled up slowly to the house, to see all of his belongings tossed out onto the street. Kasha stood in the doorway waiting on him to arrive. Marlin quickly hopped out of the car and ran up to her to see what was going on. All of his things were on the street: his shoes, clothes, laptops, every single item that Marlin cherished was scattered about down Manhattan Avenue. Several neighbors stood outside on their porches to see what all of the ruckus was about. Marlin was surely embarrassed that Kasha would do him like this. He knew that nice shit was all an act but he never imagined this to happen. He attempts to pick up his things, but when he sees Kasha running out of the house with a gas can in her hand he knows matters are about to become even worse.

"Girl, what-what the hell are you doing? And why the hell is all of my shit out on the street? What the hell is wrong with you?" Marlin yells.

"What the hell is wrong with me? What the hell is wrong with you? Don't play with me Marlin. You fucked up. You fucked up for real this time! You can kiss your kids goodbye. You will never see Christopher and Jamal anymore!" Kasha rants as she goes for the fully loaded gas can and drenches it all over Marlin's belongings and starts a fire.

"Kasha, Kasha, you f-ing bitch, what the hell are you doing?!!! So this is how we are handling things now. You're just going to torch all my shit. This is not 'Waiting to Exhale,' and you damn sure aren't Angela Bassett," Marlin yells as he slowly watches all of his prized possessions go up in flames.

"That'll teach you to cheat on me! I gave you everything, Marlin. But you took it for granted. You will never find a woman that will take care of you like I did. Go back to that whore you slept with because I am through with you!" Kasha yells, as she goes back into the house and slams the door.

There was nothing that Marlin could do. All of his worldly possessions had gone up in smoke along with his self-respect, dignity and pride. What else did he have left? A few moments of pleasure had cost him a lifetime of regret. He couldn't believe he'd just lost what was so special to him. Were a few nights spent in a hotel with Monica worth all of this? He would have to get revenge for all the damage that she caused in his life. But little did he know trouble was coming alright, but not in the direction he would like. Nor for the person he was seeking.

Chapter 14
I'm Baaaaaaaack!!!!!

Monica is having a normal conversation with her friends Rachel and Tina, like on any other normal day at work. They are in the break room sipping on some Tim Horton's coffee before leaving for home. This is when Monica almost knocks over her cup of Ice Mocha. She gets the biggest shock of her life once she spots what she believes is Keith walking into the room.

"So what do you think about that, Monica?" Tina asks Monica about a recent event in the White House.

Monica doesn't answer as her eyes are locked on Keith walking across the room to a far away table. He greets a few co-workers and begins chatting with his old friend Bradley. He periodically looks up at Monica with a huge grin upon his face. Stricken with fear, she tries to play it off like she does not see him. Trying to get back to the conversation, she feels a strange chill run down her spine, as if his eyes could pierce her soul. Feeling a little nervous, she decides to distract herself by pulling out her iPhone and checking her messages.

"Hello, Monica!" Rachel said as she snatches the phone away from her.

"What, Rachel?" Monica asks a little frustrated.

"Girl, would you put down your phone and answer the question? Uh, is that who I think it is?" Rachel questions.

"What are you talking about?"

"Come on, don't try and act like you don't see Keith sitting across the room. What the hell is he doing here?"

"Rachel, I don't know okay. Look, I'm going to run to the ladies room," Monica tries to sneak out to the restroom without being noticed by Keith. Once she steps into the empty bathroom she shuts the door behind her and takes a long hard look at herself in the mirror. Where did Keith come from? He was supposed to be gone far away? He was supposed to be a distant memory in her mental rolodex. How did he get here? How did he get out? What would he do to her now that he was out? Her life had been getting out of hand ever since she encountered Keith's presence. How could things get worse? Snapping out of things, she decided to call Ashleigh's school to check up on her before picking her up early. She searched her Louie Vuitton purse for her phone but couldn't find it. In a panic, she began frantically looking through her purse. Where could it be? Irritated, she dumps the purse out over the counter only to find her phone is still missing.

"Where the hell is that thing?" she quietly says to herself.

"Damn, it must still be in the break room, shit!" As she collected her items and placed them back into her purse she slowly made her way back to the room. After spotting her phone at the table she is greeted by Keith who is standing right in front of her.

"Hello, honey. How are you? Long time no see, huh? Yeah, you left your phone sitting right here on the table. If I wasn't here, someone could have come in and stole it. Good thing I was still here," Keith says as he hands Monica her phone and holds his hands out for a hug.

"Keith, what the hell are you doing here? How did you even get –"

"My wife took care of that little situation and I am glad that she did. Now that me and you can catch up where we left –"

"KEITH!!!! There are no us! When will you get that through your head, damn!" she yells at him.

"MONICA, you cannot deny what we have. What about all the money and expensive shit I bought you. You're just going to forget about all of that!"

"I didn't ask you to do any of that, you did it on your own. So why the hell are you tripping now? I don't owe you anything."

"Oh baby, you're right, you're right. We've known each other far too long to be arguing. Let's work this out."

"Work what out? Keith I have to go, excuse me," Monica shoves Keith out of the way and he stumbles onto a nearby table.

Keith reaches for Monica's arm but she pulls it back.

"We have been working together at this company for far too long. I've always wanted you and I damn sure know that you always wanted me. Or all of this wouldn't have happened. Stop running away from what we have Monica. There is something between us and I am not ready to give that up." Keith confesses to her, as he stares deeply into her eyes.

"Keith, will you please let me go. There is nothing between us. I have somewhere I need to be right now," Monica replies, as she brushes past Keith and exits the room, leaving Keith standing alone.

"I won't give up on us, Monica. I'll never give up on what we have," he quietly whispers to himself before he too exits the room.

Chapter 15
Leave No Witnesses

On a late Friday evening, Marlin is driving home from a long hectic day of work. As he taps his fingers on the steering wheel, he presses play on his dual CD player. He sings along with the song, "I Feel like Dying" by Lil' Wayne. The song resonates over the speakers in his Lexus. Marlin pulls up at a red light and checks his inside mirror to see a pile of papers from work sitting on his briefcase in the backseat. He quietly sighs to himself and wipes his brow thinking about the heavy load of work before him. Just as the light changes he receives a text that reads, "Meet me at Mayark Bridge at midnight. Come alone, Monica."

"Monica! What the hell does this chick want? After all the shit she caused me. Oh yeah, I'll meet you alright. I got something for that ass, most definitely," Marlin said to himself, as he tapped the glove department where he kept his heater.

Marlin pressed on the gas and swung a left from the far right lane. He bypassed almost every red light he saw as he raced to get to Mayark Bridge. Already a few minutes behind schedule he was in an immediate anticipation to see Monica. As his back wheels pulled up to the garage of the Mayark Bridge, Marlin reached for his heater and cut off his ignition.

He made his way through the dark midnight air and up to the steep bridge to put his plan into action. All the while, he never once took his hand off of his heater, which was securely placed in the back waist of his pants. He begins to call out to the dark anonymous figure in front of him. He calls out to whom he believes is Monica, yet she doesn't turn around.

"Monica, Monica! Hey trick. I know you fucking hear me! You know you got a lot of nerve coming into my life and trying to fuck up things between me and my family," he yells as he approaches her. He places his hands on her shoulders but as she turns around Marlin is in for a huge surprise. The person he has assumed it to be is indeed not Monica, but instead it is Keith standing before him.

"Sooo, you're the one who took my Monica away from me!" Keith rants as he shoves Marlin's hand away.

"Man, what are you talking about and who in the hell are you?!" Marlin questions Keith.

"Excuse me, how do you even know me?" he questions Keith.

"You took Monica from me, now I'm going to take what's mine," Keith threatens, as he pulls out a .45 caliber pistol and raises it to Marlin's chest.

"Oh hold up man, what the hell is your problem? I don't even want that hoe. You can have her. It's not even that damn serious not over some damn broad. Come on man." Marlin tries to plead with Keith as he is slowly reaches for his gun. He pulls out his gun and lets one go in Keith's chest.

"Yeah nigga, take that shit. You tryna mess with a nigga and shit... Dude you don't know me. I'm from the eastside. Shoot me nigga, I'm not scared! I ain't scared of dying," Marlin threats to Keith, but he is not injured.

"If you were a real ass nigga you would've come pre-pared," Keith says, as he lifts up his shirt to reveal his bullet-proof vest. Marlin starts to back up with one hand on his gun and another across his chest.

"If its one thing I can't stand, it is a punk ass nigga. It's a punk ass nigga that's trying to steal my girl," Keith states, as he raises his gun to Marlin's head, shooting him. Marlin stumbles and falls to the ground, as the bridge begins to shake. Gasping for air, Marlin places his left hand against his chest. He struggles to speak, as his life escapes him. Keith stares at his lifeless body and tosses it over the Mayark Bridge.

*****

A couple of weeks later, Monica has begun to live a normal life. She hasn't run into Keith at work since she was transferred to a separate division. Monica has been trying to rid herself of everything that has anything to do with Keith and that insane situation she was once in. But as she is opening her car door, two police officers slowly approach her.

"Ms. Clayton, may I have a word with you? My name is Officer Lewis and this here is my partner Officer Johnson. We just wanted to speak with you about the whereabouts of Marlin Jackson? He has been missing for two and a half weeks. We believe you were the last to be seen with him."

"Oh my goodness, I didn't even know he was missing. I swear I haven't heard anything. I don't"

"Well, please give us a call if you hear anything," Officer Johnson states as he hands Monica a business card.

"Uh, I sure will. Thank you officer," Monica says, as a sudden fear came over her body. What could have happened to Marlin? Why was he missing? She was hoping that the worse wouldn't be true. He couldn't be dead. Why would the police want to speak with her? Monica really hoped that Marlin being missing had nothing to do with Keith. But why would Keith want to hurt Marlin? All of this was just too much for her to deal with at the moment.

Monica drives home to her condominium and makes her way into the building. Ashleigh was staying over at

Rachel's for the weekend. This allowed Monica to indulge in some personal time. As Monica is making her way up the stairs to her home, Keith steps out behind her and stops her from opening the door to her apartment.

"Monica!"

"KEITH!!" Monica screams out of fear.

"What the hell are you doing here? Why can't you just leave me alone?"

"I took care of everything so we can be together. There will be no one standing in our way."

"Keith what the hell is you talking about?"

"I know that I messed up and it led you into the arms of another man but I promise you there will be no mo..."

"Tell me Keith, do you know anything about Marlin being missing for two weeks?"

"I took care of him just like I'm going to take care of you, take care of us. I did this for us."

"Keith what the hell is wrong with you?"

"What the hell is wrong with you?!? I'm sick and tired of chasing after your ungrateful selfish ass! You should appreciate all that I am doing to secure you with a good ass man. But you'd rather be an unappreciative little bitch."

"I'm going to call the police. I have told you..."

"Shut up!" Keith says as he slaps Monica.

As Monica screams out, a nearby nosy neighbor steps out of their door to see what the arguing was about. Monica turns her head to say"Call the police!"

"You should learn to appreciate a good man like me. I am a damn good man. Bitches like you make it hard for men like us to want to be with you," Keith says as he is strongly holding on to Monica's arm.

"Keith what the hell is wrong with you?"

"It's me Shanna. Why couldn't you see what you had in me?"

"Who the hell is Shanna?" Monica questions, as she tries to loosen Keith's grip on her arm.

"You are? What are you talking about Shanna?" Keith says, as he finally releases his grip on Monica.

"I'm not Shanna. I'm Monica. I don't know who the hell this Shanna is."

"You're not Shanna?"

"No. I'm Monica. Monica Clayton. Who is Shanna?"

"Don't you remember? We dated back in college until you cheated and left me for that quarterback punk at Cal U? How could you forget what we had?" Keith reminisces.

As Monica walks backward toward the nearby neighbor's door in case things turn dangerous, Keith begins to stare at Monica.

"You aren't Shanna?"

"No, I'm not," Monica says forcefully.

"But you look just like her. You have her eyes, her lips, her hair and your skin is so perfect. I'm sorry. I'm so sorry. All this time I thought you were Shanna Lewis, a girlfriend back in college that broke my heart. I vowed that I would get her back in my life through any means necessary. I'm so sorry, Monica," he said as he tried to raise his hand to touch Monica's face. She held up her hand to block Keith's presence.

A few moments later, a few police officers walked into the building. They immediately saw that the disturbance was between Keith and Monica.

"What's going on here ma'am? We got a call at this location about a possible domestic dispute," the police officer stated.

"Yes, my name is Monica Clayton, and I have a restraining order against this gentleman."

"Sir, I assure you there is nothing going on here. It was just a little argument that got a little out of hand. We had a little misunderstanding is all? All is well officers."

"May I see some ID?"

"I'm sure officer there is no need to..."

"Show me some identification!"

Keith reaches into his pocket and hands over his driver's license to the officer.

"Hands behind your back and you have the right to remain silent," the officer states to Keith.

"What's going on here?" Keith questions.

"You're under arrest for violation of a restraining order against Shanna Lewis and Monica Clayton and the murder of Alexis Holdings."

"Murder, officer what are you talking about?" Monica questions, as she is peeking her head out of a neighbor's apartment.

"Yes, we've been doing a background check on this guy since you and another woman had restraining orders placed on him. He murdered one of his stalker victims a few months ago.

So it's a good thing we got this guy before things got any worse," the officer says before taking Keith away in the squad car.

Monica stood in complete disbelief as she watched the police drive down the street. How could he have done all of these things, yet hide this from his wife and child? Did he live a double life? She couldn't believe how incredibly insane this man was. Who the hell was Shanna Lewis in the first damn place? Who was Alexis Holdings? How did she die? Did he murder all of the women he couldn't have? Monica just couldn't believe that things have gotten so out of hand with one man. She had no idea that this man was this damn crazy! All she did know was that Keith needed help. Did she really remind him of an old girlfriend to the point that he truly believed that she was someone she wasn't. It was pretty clear that Keith was a fatal attraction type. She had to do something to get him out of her life once and for all before it was too late. Hopefully, this would be the last she would ever see of Keith.

Chapter 16
Traffic Jams

I t is a late rainy evening. The storm had just passed but the chill is still in the air. Two women sit in an unlicensed Lincoln Navigator outside the Unique Hair Design Beauty Salon.

"So, are you really going to do this girl? Do you really think it's worth it?" the woman asks to her partner in the car.

"Of course I am. I have to take this bitch out. She messed over my family. I can't stand home wreckers. This chick has got to pay. I can't stand females who think the rules don't apply to them. It's time to fuck this hoe up," the female driver says.

"Yeah girl, I can't stand home wreckers neither, woman like her give us good women a bad name," the other female voice says.

*****

Monica is coming out of the Unique Hair Design Beauty Salon after getting her hair styled by one of her favorite stylists. She pulls out her keys to get into her BMW and has no idea what is about to happen. The two drivers of the anonymous truck pull up behind Monica as she is sitting at a red light. Monica thinks nothing of it until she drives off and the truck behind her has turned on its headlights. The glare from the lights almost blinds and impairs her peripheral vision.

"Who the hell is that with those bright ass lights?" Monica thinks to herself. As she is preparing for a left hand turn on Decatur Avenue, the Navigator behind her picks up its speed and starts following her. She begins to notice the unknown vehicle tailing her. So she turns onto the freeway to try and get away.

"Oh, she thinks she is going to get away. I got something for her ass," the driver of the Lincoln Navigator says.

Monica switches lanes and the car begins to rear-end her. The faster she drives, the faster they drive. Monica tries to pick up her phone to call Rachel and tell her that someone is following her, but as she reaches for the phone she is struck from behind a second time.

"Yeah, I got that ho. She's going to get what the hell she deserves tonight. We're ending this ho's life tonight!" the driver brags, after hitting Monica's car.

"Oh my goodness, who the hell is this hitting me? "

Monica tries to speed up to lose the attacker so she merges onto another lane on the freeway. But the faster she drives the faster the driver of the truck gains on her. She begins to fear for her life. Who could this be tail ending her? Why would someone want to kill her? The more she presses on the gas the more the driver behind her picks up in speed. Monica decides to get off the freeway and get back on the residential streets. As she is panicking, Monica tries to pick up the phone to call the police, but she doesn't realize that she is approaching a railroad track. She looks up after hearing the whistle of a train. Hoping that her brakes don't fail, she sees the following vehicle in her inside view mirror. Right at that moment, she was at a point of desperation. Does she stop to avoid the train, or try her best to make it across to keep from being rear-ended by this truck that is rapidly approaching? The faster the train came, the faster the truck went. Monica was stuck. She was at a crossroads. If she tried to make it across before the train came there was a chance that she would be killed immediately. But if she stopped she would be taking a chance on letting the truck hit her again and kill her upon impact. She tries to slam on the breaks to avoid hitting the train, but for some reason, she can't stop. A blinking light inside her car reads, "Check Brakes." This couldn't be happening right now. Monica presses on her brakes again but hears a loud grinding noise. As she tries her best to stop the car, the Navigator gained momentum and rammed into her car once again. The Navigator pushed Monica's car onto the tracks while the train was approaching. She tried to move her vehicle out of the way but her doors became jammed and her seatbelt wouldn't unfasten. Monica was in a panic, and didn't know what to do. In a race to save her life, she broke the windshield to climb out of the car, just as the train collided with her car. The train pushed it down the tracks a quarter of a mile. Monica rolls onto the concrete and ends up face down. She is unable to move and is lying unconscious on the ground.

"Hell yeah, we got that bitch! I told you we weren't about to let that ho live tonight!" Kasha rejoiced, making a U-turn the other way down the street.

"Are you crazy? You could have killed her, what is the matter with you, Kasha? I think we went too far. I thought we were just going to scare her, not kill her! Granted I wanted to get back at her for what she did but I don't know if we should've tried to end her life," Rochelle said breathing hard.

"Girl, you're too soft. That ho needed to be taught a fucking lesson. I bet she won't mess with another woman's man now. I lost my child's father because of that ratchet mess. So excuse me if I'm a just a little vexed right now, Rochelle," Kasha shouts, as she is driving away from the scene.

Twenty minutes passes before anyone sees Monica's unconscious body lying on the ground. A passerby slows to a stop and immediately phones Emergency once he realizes Monica is unable to breathe. The EMS arrives at the scene of Rosin and Lennox. They try to feel for a pulse and placed her body on the gurney. She gets rushed to the Riverview Hospital with no certainty that she will pull through. Technicians try to revive her so that she doesn't fall into a coma. Who could believe all of this occurred because of her past wrongdoings. Was messing with married men worth losing your life? If Monica wanted to set a responsible example for Ashleigh, she would need to change her ways. This was a true wake-up call that she needed to change her ways and live right. It was time to turn over a new leaf in life.

Chapter 17
The Wake-Up Call

A few weeks have passed and Monica has begun to recuperate. While she sleeps the faint sounds of the ventilator beeps. A slight knock at the door awakes her. She opens her eyes slowly to see Rachel and Ashleigh standing in front of her with an oversized teddy bear and flowers. Monica slowly rises up to give her daughter a hug. Her daughter has tears running down her face as she watches her mother sitting in the hospital bed in pain.

"What happened mommy?" Ashleigh questioned sadly.

"Oh, mommy was in an accident but she is alright. You don't have to worry about me."

"Um, go lie down Ashleigh. I'll be over there in a moment," Rachel tells Ashleigh.

Ashleigh goes to lie down on the couch across the room.

"Monica, what the hell happened? Are you alright? Did you say that someone was following you?" Rachel asked hysterically.

"All I remember was someone rear-ending me, and I almost got crushed by a train."

"Oh my God, I am glad you're alright. Who do you think would do such a thing to you?"

"I don't know. I honestly feel it is God punishing me for all the pain I've caused. You always told me the drama I did would come back to me. I don't know, I've done a lot of thinking while being in this hospital. I've been doing some long hard thinking," Monica comments.

"Well, as sorry as I feel for you. I do have to say that this whole thing has gotten pretty out of hand. I've been more of a mother to Ashleigh than you and I don't have any kids. Come on Monica, that isn't right. Your daughter's birthday is next week. Do you even remember how old she'll be? I mean running around with all these different men. You don't know if these men had anything girl."

"I know what I did was wrong. That's why I made a vow to GOD and my daughter to live right. I really am trying to change and live for Ashleigh. It would break my heart if she grew up and started acting like this. She deserves better and I need to give her better," Monica said as she stared over at her daughter who was sound asleep on the couch.

"Yes, thank you Monica. All of this drama was just crazy. I told you all that mess would catch up with you someday. You never did listen. Now look at yourself sitting up here in the hospital when you could be in the comfort of your own home."

"I know Rachel. I know. Things are really going to be different from now on. I-"

"Hey, hey, this has been the news story I've been following for a while now," Rachel says as she turns up the volume on the TV screen. A news anchor on the Channel 7 news is reporting a breaking news story.

"Police have finally identified the body found in the Mayark River some months ago. Action News Reporter Rhonda Wilson has more, Rhonda," Francesca Monroe reports.

"Yes, Francesca, police have finally identified the body found some months ago in the Mayark River to be 27 year-old Marlin Turner. He was a computer consultant. Authorities identified the victim after finding his vehicle parked in the Mayark structure some twenty feet away from the bridge. According to autopsy reports, he suffered gunshots to the head. There is still an investigation underway as to who murdered Turner. The next of kin have already been notified. He leaves behind a wife and two little boys. The wife of the victim was too distraught for words. Reporting live at the Mayark Bridge, I'm Rhonda Wilson, Channel 7 Action News."

As Monica and Rachel are listening to this tragic news story Monica is in complete shock. She couldn't believe that Marlin was actually murdered. Did Keith Jackson have something to do with the murder of Marlin Turner? How could Monica have allowed herself to get caught up in all of this madness? She knew that in order for her not to wind up the next murder victim on the news, she knew things had to change.

Chapter 18
My Pain, Your Misery

Monica has reached a full recovery since the accident. She has had time to enjoy her time spent with her daughter. She also has decided to leave the state of Maryland and move to Florida for a fresh start within the next year or so. Monica will be relocating her job to the Shears & Perry Marketing Miami Division. All of the tragedy and turmoil she has caused has spiraled out of control, thus making her live a life she never dreamed of. But she knew that if she really wanted to move past all of what she has done. She had to get to the root of the problem first. Rachel comes out of the kitchen with a couple of cups of coffee. The two sit on the couch while watching an episode of *The View*.

"You know Rach, I'm just glad that things are starting to turn around for me. I don't know how my life got so out of control."

"I know. It's because you don't listen. I told you not to mess with Keith, girl. But Keith wasn't the first guy you messed around with. You've been doing this sort of thing since college. I mean, why'd you do it? Did you do it to get men? Get women mad at you? And if you didn't know, these women out here aren't playing. You can't just go sleeping with their husbands and think they won't do anything about it."

"I know. I always told myself that I'd get back at men for what they did to me."

"What men? What did men do to you?" Rachel questions.

"He left me, he left us, Rachel. How could you forget what he did?" Monica questions with a quiver in her voice.

"Who left you?"

"Donovan. Donovan Lewis."

"Ashleigh's father…? You are still fuming over what he did to you? That was over five years ago."

"But he left me for no damn reason while I was five months pregnant with Ashleigh. He left me to go be with another woman. Now he has a new family and doesn't want to acknowledge her. I didn't make her by myself. I am tired of raising Ashleigh by myself."

"Monica! I know what Donovan did to you back in college was foul, but come on; you can't blame the actions of one guy on the entire male species. You have got to let go of that pain, or you will never move on.

Don't allow a man that has moved on with his life affect your future. You deserve better. Ashleigh deserves better. Look at yourself, Monica. Although you got pregnant with Ashleigh you still managed to go back to school to get your MBA. You are now Chief Executive Officer at Shears & Perry marketing and a successful young, black woman. How many women can say that? You need to let go of all of that pain and be there for your little girl. She needs you. She needs you to be alive and healthy. You will be alright. But you can't bring misery to others because of the pain that you feel, especially pain caused over five years ago. Let it go, girl. Let it go!" Rachel advises Monica.

Chapter 19
Jeremy

~Six Months Later~

Monica has fully recovered since the tragic accident and she has begun to change her ways. She has decided to devote all of her time and attention to raising her daughter Ashleigh. Monica is outside of PS. 116 Elementary School waiting for her daughter to come running to her. The school was surrounded by children of all ages, from kindergarten to fifth grade. Once Ashleigh spotted Monica she ran to her with open arms.

"Mommie, Mommie!" Ashleigh squeals with delight.

"Hey Ashleigh, how was school today?"

"It was so much fun! My class is having a party to-morrow and everybody in my class has to bring snacks to eat," Ashleigh states happily.

"Well alright, let's go to the grocery store." Ashleigh and Monica head to the store to purchase some snacks for the party. The grocery store is surprisingly not as busy as it usually is. As they are shopping Ashleigh has her eyes set on the cookies and cupcakes.

Meanwhile, Monica, who is looking down the aisle, wondrously spots a rather tall man standing in front of her with a shopping cart full of food. He is dark brown, has a nice athletic build, sandy-brown eyes and a smile to die for. The man looks up and notices Monica. The two share an instant attraction.

At that moment Monica had to know who this irresistible mystery man was who resembled a popular basketball player. But then she had to ask herself if getting to know another man worth it with her horrific track record? She already endured the loss of one and the criminalization of another. Something inside her, screamed yes. Yes! 100% all of the way, as the gentleman made his way closer to her, Monica started to feel a sense of nervousness come over her.

"Hello, miss. I couldn't help but notice that you were checking me out."

"Excuse me, but you are mistaken. You were checking 'me' out. I don't pursue men," Monica explains arrogantly.

"Oh well, let's just say that we were both checking each other out. My name is Jeremy Stuart. What's your name, lovely?" he questions with a sexy grin on his face, exposing his perfect, bright white teeth.

Monica shakes his hand and replies flirtatiously, "Monica, Monica Clayton," she suddenly snaps back into reality when Ashleigh taps her on the back.

"Ma!"

"Huh, yes, Ashleigh."

"I want to get the rest of the food for the party, Ma," Ashleigh whines, pulling on Monica's arm.

"Okay, hold on honey. Well, I have to go now, Jeremy Stuart."

"Alright Ms. Monica Clayton, maybe our paths will cross again," Jeremy says.

"I'm sure they will. Bye now." Monica turns to follow Ashleigh towards the party snacks.

Monica knew that she should've been more concerned with her daughter's class party, but for some strange reason, she couldn't take her mind off Jeremy. There was something about him she found extremely attractive. Whatever it was, Monica hoped she'd somehow run into him again. He was definitely worth remembering.

After they came from the grocery store, Monica pulls up into the parking lot of her condominium. As she is helping Ashleigh out of her booster seat in the backseat, she notices a man getting out of his car just a couple of spaces down. He looks familiar. It couldn't be...it was

Jeremy getting out of his Miata, groceries in hand. Monica and Ashleigh walk towards him slowly.

"Oh my goodness, are you stalking me? How'd you know where I live Jeremy?" Monica asks.

"What? I'm not following you, and I am not a stalker. I live here, too. I just moved into this building a few weeks ago," Jeremy answers.

"Really, I didn't notice. Well, I guess we will see a lot of each other then, huh?"

Jeremy chuckles at Monica's question. "Yeah, I guess we will then." Jeremy agrees as he closes the trunk to his car. He follows Monica and her daughter to the door. Jeremy, being the gentleman that he is, opens the door for the both of them to walk inside the building.

The next day, after taking an overly excited Ashleigh to school for her party, Monica, comes back home and decides to do a few loads of laundry. She goes downstairs to the Laundromat located on the 1st floor of her building. The room was filled with people waiting for the dryer to finish their clothes. As Monica is sorting her clothes and tossing them into the washer machine, she receives a kiss on the neck and a gentle hug.

"Hey beautiful, how are you this morning?" Jeremy greets her surprisingly. She turns around to see him standing behind her.

"Hey you, I'm beginning to think you really are following me," Monica says jokingly.

"No, no. Just a coincidence, that's all. I'm just waiting on the dryer to finish up. I washed earlier. How's the little lady doing?"

"If you're referring to Ashleigh, she's at school. Her class is having a party, so she's pretty excited."

"Oh, okay. Um, what are you doing this weekend?" Jeremy questions.

"Why, Mr. Stuart?" she questions sternly, while adding the fabric softener in with the load of clothes.

"I maybe wanted to ask you out on a date, that's if you're not doing anything Saturday evening?"

"Where are we going?" Monica begins to warm up.

"Oh, so now you're going to act like you're not as interested in me as I am in you," Jeremy states as he is taking a seat.

Monica laughs, "I'll have to find a sitter for Ashleigh but alright Jeremy, we can go out." Monica confirms.

"That's what I'm talking about. Okay, I'll be at your apartment around seven. Let me know if you get a sitter for your daughter. My clothes are done so I guess I'll be heading back up to my apartment now," Jeremy states as he retrieves his clothes from the dryer machine. As he leaves the room Monica follows him with her eyes until he is out of sight. Although she tried to fight the feeling, deep down she knew there was something about this man that was special. The touch from his embrace made her shudder with desire. The warmth from his kiss on her neck made her burn with passion.

Later That Saturday Evening

Monica and Jeremy are finally on their date at Steve's Soul Food Place. As they are eating, she decides to ask Jeremy some very interesting questions.

"You know, Monica, I must admit that you are certainly working the hell out of that black dress. I might not be able to contain myself." Jeremy laughs as his eyes are fixated on Monica's lovely assets. The black silk see-through dress gathered a few other male's attention, as well.

"Thank you, Jeremy. You look pretty damn good, too. I think we make one pretty sexy-ass couple," Monica agrees.

"Um, with that being said, I want to know three things. Don't get offended but, are you married, are you on the down low and do you have HIV or any STD's?"

Jeremy taken by surprise with the questions Monica asks spits out his Ciroc.

"Excuse me?"

"I'm asking you seriously? In this day and age a woman has to know these things. So, um hello are you going to answer the questions?"

"Well to be honest with you…no…no and um no…"

"…Why would you ask me that, Monica?"

"You would be surprised at the things I've dealt with in the past. I just want to be safe that I don't have to deal with any of that crazy mess anymore."

"Oh, I understand. No, I am certainly not married. I never have been, but I would welcome the opportunity. I don't even have any children. I am certainly not gay; not at all girl! Lastly, I get tested pretty frequently so I'm sure I'm clean. What else do you want to know about me?"

"What do you do for a living?"

"Well, right now I'm on vacation. I use to play for the Sinai Raptors. But since I injured my leg, I'm on an extended vacation. I'm going to go play for the Miami Falcons in Florida in the next few months,"

"Oh really? Wow, that's cool. I am actually moving to Florida, as well. I'm taking over the Miami division as new CEO so I'm pretty damn excited. That means more money for me and Ashleigh."

"Congratulations. Damn! Beauty and brains! Is there anything that you can't do, Monica? If you don't mind me asking, what happened to Ashleigh's father?"

"Oh well, her father, Donovan walked out on me when I was four or five months pregnant and decided to go impregnate another woman, marry her and forget we ever existed."

"Oh, I'm sorry. Well it's his loss. But if he wouldn't have left, I wouldn't have the opportunity to meet you."

"Well, aren't you quite the charmer?"

"I'm really interested in getting to know you. Next time we should bring your little girl with us."

"You already know it'll be a next time, huh?"

"I'm pretty confident in my skills. Why don't we take this back to my place?"

"What do you have in mind?"

"Anything, we could watch a movie, listen to some music, whatever you want to do."

Something in Monica knew she shouldn't go back to a man's place on the first date but it was so easy to get lost in Jeremy's deep dark eyes that she soaked up anything he said. Just imagining what he would look like undressed ran through her mind. She couldn't stop dreaming of running her hands down his sexy chest or wondering how he felt inside of her. Monica wasn't trying to bring back her wild ways of sleeping with men on the first night. After all, she had a daughter to take care of. What example would she be setting for Ashleigh by doing that? But on the same hand, it had been several months since her last sexual encounter, so she burned with an itch that desperately needed to be scratched.

"You ready to go back to my place?"

"Um, sure…"

The two leave the restaurant and head back to Jeremy's apartment. As Monica reaches his apartment, an overwhelming feeling of nervousness comes over her. She wanted desperately to remain a lady and not give into the temptations of her desires that would lead her to sleeping with Jeremy on the first night. This time, it had to be right with a sense of decorum, respect and dignity. But how could one hold on to such strong principles when her body melted from the gentleness of his touch? She could no longer deny it, Jeremy brought out the inner-most passions Monica thought had died some time ago.

Monica is sitting on the couch while Jeremy turns on some soft R&B. Usher's "Seduction," plays over the speakers. He rubs his hand on the sides of her neck. Monica jumps suddenly.

"What's the matter? It's just me. You need to relax. I promise you I'm not a crazed maniac."

Monica laughs softly.

"So what is an NBA player doing in a place like this? I mean…I thought you guys lived in $1.3 billion houses."

"Yeah right, maybe the idiots. But I'm trying to keep my money at the end of my career. This NBA thing won't last forever. So tell me, Monica why is a sexy, successful, single woman like yourself without a man?"

"I don't know. Guess I haven't found the right one yet. What about yourself?"

"Same here, I assume. But I see things working out with you. You want to watch a movie. I think "Love Jones" is playing *On Demand.*

"Oh great, I love that movie," Monica replied.

Jeremy also knew that tonight he had to have Monica. Everything within him said yes in so many ways. He couldn't imagine her not feeling the same. She leaned her body against his while they watched the movie. Jeremy ran his fingers up and down her thigh until he reached her clitoris. She moaned with pleasure as his thumb and index finger massaged her vaginal walls. Slowly, she opened her legs to welcome him. Silently, she whispered his name. Silently she whispered all the things she wanted him to do to her. In return, he took delight in the joy he was giving to her. Overcome with emotion, Jeremy places her legs around his waist and proceeds to go to the bedroom. As he lays her down on the bed he begins to take off his shirt, exposing a nicely shaven six-pack chest. Monica knew there was no turning back from this. She tried hard to resist the temptations of sleeping with Jeremy on the first date, but somehow she knew that it would truly be worth every second of regret she'd feel in the morning. He slowly began undressing her until she was completely naked.

"Damn." It was all Jeremy could say. He quickly pulled down his pants and entered.

Monica squealed and held on tightly to his arms. There was no better feeling she could experience at this moment. The louder she screamed, the harder he worked. She couldn't believe the incredible sensation she was feeling. It was nothing she could do but enjoy the ride along the way. As he worked hard on her pussy, she could feel a cascade of water falling between her legs. No one had ever made her feel like this. Quietly, he demanded to know who was in charge and she didn't mind letting him know. After, she exploded all over his dick; she climbed on top and took the reins. She could feel

Jeremy growing larger by the second. He was letting out quiet moans and it would just be a matter of seconds before he'd bust his nut. He slowly caressed his hands up and down Monica's back and sides, making his way up to her breasts. Quickly, flipping her over, he decided to work her from the back. She screamed as he entered her. Trying to contain herself, she grabbed on to the pillow and bit down. He was working that ass like it was going out of style. This was the best dick she had received in a long time. She knew that her pussy would thank her in more than a millions ways. He brought out the absolute worse in her. Monica never imagined it'd be like this. This experience was better than anything she had ever had with Keith or Marlin. Jeremy was certainly the man for her, especially if he could fuck her like this all day every day. She'd do anything to keep this shit going. After, they exploded and were out of breath, Jeremy and Monica fell asleep in each other's arms.

*****

The next couple of days, Monica is kind of on edge because she hasn't heard anything from Jeremy. There were no phone calls, no texts, no stopping by the apartment or accidently running into each other. She was beginning to feel a little played, but how could he just toss her to the side after a night of lustful passion. She started to call him, but stopped herself as she didn't want to appear needy or clingy. After waiting for hours count-lessly by the phone Monica decides to go into work to take her mind off things.

On her way out the building, she runs into Jeremy in the elevator. He appears to look a little run down.

"Oh hey, what's up, Monica?" he tries to say excited-ly.

"What's up, what's up? What's up is I've been trying to call you for the past two days!" Monica replies angrily.

"For real, my cell phone must've been off or dead be-cause I didn't receive any phone calls. I'm sorry."

"What were you doing that you couldn't receive any calls, Jeremy? Did you even think to call me, Jeremy? You weren't even thinking about me..."

"Monica, Monica, Monica, damn will you calm down, shit! It was just one night, why are you getting yourself so worked up over nothing."

"Just one night, I can't believe you. You are..."

"First, of all, I was busy. I told you when we first got together I'd be getting ready for the season soon. I was in training camp. You need to relax; some things aren't what they seem. Sometimes, you have to be patient to get the response you're looking for. Well, I need to go get some rest. I'm going back to my room. See you later, beautiful." Jeremy explains as he gently kisses Monica on the forehead.

"I got you d-whopped," he says sing-song while the elevator lifts towards his floor.

"No you don't."

"Whatever!" he replies back a distance.

Furiously, Monica thinks his story is complete bull. She couldn't believe how he could just play her like that, like she was a one night stand. Who did he think he was? Just because he was an athlete didn't give him the right to mistreat anyone.

As the elevator reached the lobby, Monica stepped out. She pulled the belt tighter on her pea coat as she switched out of the building in her six inch stilettos. Timothy, the desk attendant, calls out to her before she exits the building.

"Monica, Monica, Ms. Clayton. Someone left a lovely gift for you the other day," Tim says as he hands Monica 12 long-stem roses, a heart-shaped box of chocolates, and with a card attached. Monica opens the card to read the note inside:

I really enjoyed our date the other day.
I think we should see more of each other.
You're an amazing woman.
-Love, Jeremy.

Monica felt a sense of warmth come over her along with guilt for snapping at Jeremy the way she did. He wasn't just blowing her off; he felt the same way she did, and that was a sigh of relief. Could she have finally found the one? He was tall, dark and handsome, successful, not married, no baggage and most importantly no drama. Things seemed to be turning around for the better, at least romantically for her. She hoped things would only get better.

*****

A few months' later things are still progressing pretty nicely between Jeremy and Monica. In fact, he has grown pretty attached to Ashleigh as well. She is even beginning to think of him as a dad. Jeremy, Monica and Ashleigh are leaving for Florida and plan on moving in together.

Chapter 20
Something in the Past

Things were changing and things were changing fast, yet for the better in Monica's life. She was finally getting to a place in her life where she was not just content but joyously happy. She has finally gotten past all the fiasco with the married men and found herself a real man. He was a real man who catered to all of her needs. He, too, was a man who acknowledged her child as his own. Monica saw good things for Ashleigh's future as well. Her daughter would start first grade in a more advanced school system. Plus, Monica had a fresh new start in a state with a high paying position, running the whole company. What could be better than being CEO of a marketing firm in Miami, FLA? Take that for a real boss lady. All was left to do was to get on that plane and kiss Baltimore, Maryland goodbye.

Awaiting the arrival of their flight, Monica and Ashleigh are standing in line at the airport waiting to board the plane.

"Hey Monica, since it's such a long line and I can see Ashleigh getting a little antsy, do you mind if we go get a few snacks to eat? You just call me when you're ready?" Jeremy says.

"Um, alright, please be careful. Please don't get lost."

"We won't, Monica! I know this place like the back of my hand. Don't worry she's in good hands," Jeremy reassures, as he and Ashleigh walk away.

Annoyed and frustrated, Monica is checking the time on her watch while someone from behind bumps into her almost knocking her down.

"Um, excuse me. You nearly knocked me over!" Monica shouts.

"Well, I think that's nothing compared to the damage you've caused me and my family," the voice says.

"What? Do I even know you?"

As Monica turns around to face the person behind her, she receives the biggest shock of her life...its Kasha standing before her.

"Oh, you remember me now huh?! Funny seeing you here, isn't this some fucked up coincidence?"

"Ugh, hi, Kasha...how are you doing?" Monica says nervously.

"How am I doing? How am I doing? How the hell do you think I'm doing? Hmm, I lost my husband because of you. I lost my marriage again because of you. I suggest you watch your back, honey, because I'll never let you forget what you've done to me and my family," Kasha proclaims, walking away.

Monica felt every butterfly floating around in her stomach at that second. Her perfect little world had just crumbled before her. She was finally at a point in her life where she could leave all of the traumatic experiences behind her but with Kasha now going to Miami as well, there was no room to relax, to breathe, or exhale. How would this affect her relationship with Jeremy? Things had just started going in the right direction. Would he get caught up in all of this madness? What about Ashleigh? Would Kasha try to hurt her daughter to get back at her?

Frozen in fear, she jumped when she felt a gentle tap on the shoulder from behind.

"Hey, Monica…"

"What!?!" she shouts.

"What's wrong, it's just us. Are you alright?" Jeremy asks holding Ashleigh's hand.

"Oh nothing…Are you ready to board the plane now?"

"Yeah, that's why we tried to hurry back. Ashleigh's pretty full too."

"Alright, well let's go."

The three of them board the plane that will take them to Florida, together. On the flight are people of all ages and races. Ashleigh has never been on a plane before and rushes to the window seat. Jeremy sits next to her, while Monica takes the aisle seat. Monica still can't take her mind off Kasha. How could she still be holding a grudge against her after all this time? Monica wasn't the cause of her husband's death. If she had known how crazy Marlin's wife really was she would've just left him alone a long time ago. No man was worth the trouble she might have been in. She is lost in thought when Jeremy tries to get her attention.

"Monica, Monica, Monica!"

"Huh, oh hey, J, what's up?"

"Are you sure you're okay? It seems as if your mind is somewhere else."

"Oh, I'm sorry, J. There is just a lot on my mind," Monica says.

"Like what?" he questions.

"Oh, it's not important right now. I'll tell you later."

"You know I've been thinking lately, I really enjoy my time with you, even my time with Ashleigh. I really like how things are progressing with us. I can see myself in this for the real long haul."

"So, what are you trying to say, Jeremy?"

"Let's just say I have something very important to ask you when we get to Miami."

Monica smiles with a look of surprise stamped upon her face. She knew exactly what he wanted to ask.

"Also, Monica, what do you think about the idea of having another baby?" he asks.

"Are you crazy? I'm not having another baby? I'm already stressed with the one I got now. Why do you ask?"

"Um, I don't know. I think we'll see in about six to seven more months," Jeremy laughs.

"Boy, what are you talking about? Hold on I'll be right back. I'm going to the ladies room."

Monica makes her way to the restroom still thinking about Jeremy's statements. It was obvious he was thinking about marriage, but did he actually want a baby? Did he want a baby of his own? Monica wasn't thrilled about the idea of bringing Ashleigh a baby brother or sister. This would be something for them to seriously discuss.

As Monica is walking out of the restroom, someone grabs her from behind and drags her back into the bathroom.

"Looks like we meet again?" Kasha says.

"What the hell are you doing? What do you want from me?" Monica asks, as she rises to her feet.

"What do you think, for the coroner to determine your cause of death through an autopsy report? You've got some nerve, bitch! How can you act like you had nothing to do with Marlin's death? You took away everything I had...my happy home, my marriage, my husband and the father of my kids," Kasha shouts while holding a razor blade to Monica's throat.

"But I didn't have anything to do with it. In fact, I was in the hospital at the time I found out about his death," Monica answers as her voice starts to crack.

"I know I was the one who put you there."

"Excuse me?"

"I was going take you out, just like you took out my man," Kasha shouts

"How long are you going to hold this against me? I was wrong for..."

"Well, how would you feel if you were working hard to take care of your family? And some other woman comes and seduces your man, fucks your man. Your man is lying to you to spend time with this woman? Your family gets torn apart because of some slut ass trick like you! Best believe I will never ever let you forget what the hell you've done to my family. I will not rest until I see the police place a white sheet over your dead body and they're stuffing you in to a body bag, please believe that. I got people all around here ready and willing to take you and your family out, "Kasha threatens Monica, as she begins to exit the room and head back to the seating area.

Monica knew that Kasha was serious about everything she said. She just didn't see how going through all of this would bring Marlin back. It seemed as if things were getting slightly out of hand. All she wanted to do was mend things with Kasha and move on with her life.

Chapter 21
...The Bones Fell Out of YOUR Closet

Monica finally touched grounds in the hot, sunny city of Miami. She was so excited to be turning over a new leaf. She had her baby girl with her, along with her new man and her new job all within arm's reach. What woman could ask for more? Monica was too consumed with joy to even give Kasha a second thought. Jeremy pulled up to a mansion-style home in the neighborhood of South Beach. As Monica got out of the car, her mouth nearly dropped to the floor. Once he opened the door to the exotic South Beach mansion, she thought that, the house was something out of a fairytale with 5 bedrooms, a home theater, indoor and outdoor pools along with a Jacuzzi to fit at least ten people. Monica never thought in a million years that a man would ever have her living in the lap of luxury.

"Oh my goodness, J, this place is huge! How much did this place cost you? Now this is a baller's house."

"Yes, it is roughly around $1.3 million, why?"

"Are you sure you can afford it?" Monica questions.

"Can I afford it? Girl I'm a baller! Don't you think I would ever have bought it if I couldn't afford it? Now I want you and Ashleigh to get settled into your new home…"

"What did you do with your condo back in Maryland? Did you sell it?"

"No, I am leasing it out right now," Jeremy says as his iPhone beeps and he realizes that he is getting a very important call.

"Oh well, this is my general manager I have to go but I'll be back later to discuss that important "thing" we talked about on the plane, babe."

"Alright, that's fine. I have to go to work later anyway. Be careful hon. I'll miss you," Monica says, planting a few kisses on Jeremy's lips before he walks out the door.

"Hey, honey, you like the new house?" Monica asks her daughter.

"Yeah, this house is huge!"

"Yes, it is. Let's go find your bedroom."

"Okay," Ashleigh says grasping her mother's hand.

While Monica and Ashleigh search around the house, Jeremy is on his way to Industrial Parkway to meet with a few unfriendly faces. He pulls up to what looks like an abandoned building.

"1931 Industrial Parkway, but this place looks deserted. This has got to be the wrong address here," Jeremy says out loud. He gets out of the vehicle to see if there was anyone around he could speak to. He approaches the building and is greeted by a 300 lb dark-skinned bouncer guarding the entry.

"May I help you out?"

"I was told to meet Mr. Isis at this location."

"You got an appointment? Mr. Isis don't see nobody without an appointment," the bouncer claims.

"Yes, at around 3p.m., my name is Jeremy…"

"Alright go in. I hope I see you on the way out. Not everybody makes it out alive with Mr. Isis."

"Uh, okay, Thanks man. Where is he at?" Jeremy asks fearfully.

Once Jeremy enters the building and the bouncer closes the door behind him, there is no light inside the building. He is led down a long, dark pathway that eventually leads to a door. It is the only door in the entire hallway, so he assumes Mr. Isis must be on the other side of it. Slowly he knocks on the door and hears the faint voice of a gentleman again requesting his name. He is allowed entry and walks to the table where Mr. Isis is sitting with a couple of other people.

"Mr. Stuart, so nice of you to join us over here in Miami, as you may know we have some unfinished business to attend to about your outstanding gambling debt. Have you given any more thought to what we have talked about?" Mr. Isis states.

Mr. Isis is a small clean-cut man with a bit of an Italian accent dressed in an Armani suit with rings on almost all of his fingers. He was a business-man, or more like a loan shark who didn't take to well to people trying to short change him. Jeremy was in over his head and now he had to figure out how to stay above water or swim with the fishes.

"Yes, I have."

"Very good, Jeremy, because you know if you don't pay me my $15,000, I will kill you and your family. You have two weeks to come up with my cash or you know what will happen. My partner and I over here don't like when people don't pay up. The decision is up to you. You may be dismissed." Mr. Isis tells Jeremy.

Jeremy leaves the building with a million things on his mind. How would he keep this away from Monica? He knew what happened to those individuals that didn't pay up to Mr. Isis. But did he really want to give away a portion of his money just to keep his NBA career. He raced home to think of what he could do to come up with the money. On top of the debt he's forced to repay Jeremy had to suit up for his first game of the season against the Raptors next week.

****

Monica steps off the elevator and towards her brand new office at Shears & Perry marketing as the CEO. But when she approaches the office she notices a tall woman staring out the window. All she could think of is why was there a woman in her office and who was this woman?

"Uh, excuse me? This is my office," Monica speaks out.

"Oh, is that right? What is your name?" the woman asks with her eyes still focused outside.

"Monica-"

"Monica Clayton?" the woman questions Monica.

"Yes, how do you know my name?"

"Because best friends know their girls..." The woman says as she turns around. It is Rachel, Monica's best friend and Ashleigh's god-mother.

"Aahhh, oh my god, what are you doing here, girl?" Monica asks.

"I couldn't leave you in Miami by yourself. Girl, Lord knows what kind of craziness you would get yourself into without me?" Rachel adds.

"So tell me about this new man of yours...Jeremy?" she asks intrigued.

"Yes, girl, He is so sweet and sexy. He is one of the good ones that are left. I couldn't imagine him doing anything harmful to me or Ashleigh," she says.

****

Meanwhile, Jeremy is heading home. All he can think of is how he could pay Mr. Isis without things going too far or Monica finding out. He was next to perfection in her eyes and he intended to keep it that way. It would be demeaning to him to reveal to her the skeletons in his closet. After reaching the bedroom, Jeremy rushes through the door. He is in search of any extra money lying around. He comes across Monica's Tiffany and Co. jewelry set along with a couple of her mother's rings in a jewelry box. This was something he didn't want to do but he knew there would be a hefty price to pay if he didn't come up with the cash. Mr. Isis had the power to wipe out his bank account, end his ball career and his life. He took Monica's jewelry out of the box and shoved it quickly into his pocket. There was one thing he did luck up on. He was dating a CEO of a very prestigious marketing firm. So if by chance he happened to lose all of the millions he worked hard for, he'd be taken care of handsomely by the wealth Monica would soon accrue.

Jeremy placed the box back on the mantle as he heard the side door open and slam close; Monica was home. He stuffed a small velvet box into his pocket and went downstairs.

"How is my lady doing today?" he asked.

"I'm exhausted. Everything is crazy at work," Monica says as she tosses her briefcase on the couch and kicks off her heels.

"But what about you, you're playing in your first big game of the season in a couple of days. Are you ready?" she asks.

"Oh, I was born ready. I am Jeremy 'Mr. Unstoppable' Stuart. But are you ready for this?" he questions. Jeremy pulls out a small box with an emerald cut diamond engagement ring. Monica's mouth drops as tears of joy begin to well up in her eyes. Never in her wildest imagination would she see herself marrying the man of her dreams. Jeremy was everything she embodied in a mate. He was caring, loving, patient, and most importantly good with Ashleigh. After all, the men she has encountered in the past, none of them had ever captivated her heart in such a way.

"Of course I'll marry you! Yes, oh my God! I'm so excited. I can't believe I'm going to be Mrs. Jeremy Stuart! I love you so much," she says, giving Jeremy a hug and a kiss on the cheek.

"I'm glad. I'm glad. I really love you too, Monica," he says.

"I have to tell everybody, I'm getting married!" she says, waving her left hand in the air.

"Now, I think we should go out to eat to celebrate our engagement. How about we go to Celeste?"

"Oh, yes, I've been waiting to try out that restaurant."

"Then Celeste it is." Jeremy reaches out for Monica and gives her a tight squeeze.

"I really don't know where I'd be right now if it weren't for you," he admits before they start to head out to the car. Finally, Monica would soon become a married woman. After all she has been through she has truly found the one for her.

Chapter 22
I Don't Know Her!

After Jeremy has celebrated a victory win with the team, he heads back to his hotel room. Once inside, there is a big surprise waiting for him. He sees a woman sitting on his bed. She looks up and smiles. Jeremy is in complete shock. How could someone have gotten access to his room? Who was this female and why was she in is room? What did she want?

"Why hello, number 49? Good game," the woman says rising up from the bed exposing her mini-skirt as she walks toward him.

"What the hell are you doing? And why are you here?" Jeremy questions.

"Well, Mr. Jeremy Stuart. I'm Kasha Turner."

"How did you get in here? I'm going to need you to leave," he says.

"Shh! Shh! Before you get too far into specifics, let me say this. A little birdie told me that you're up the ass for

15 g's. Now if you don't want your lovely girlfriend Monica to find out. I suggest you comply with my demands and no one finds out about the nearly bankrupt NBA ballplayer with the close to perfect life."

"Wait, how do you know all of this? Are you a stalker, FBI, CIA, what, because I'm about to call the police on you for breaking and entering. So I suggest you comply with me."

"Um, no, no, no honey. You see I'm Mr. Isis' close personal friend and he told me all about you and your college loan debt and how you damn near gave up your entire life to play pro ball. So, like I said, if you don't want your girl to find out, I suggest you drop those drawers," She says placing her finger over his lips. He quickly moves it away.

"I don't care who sent you. I'm not sleeping with you. You can't coerce me into sleeping with you Kasha or whatever the hell your name is. That's blackmail," Jeremy argues.

"Black male, white male, they're all the same to me," she says, removing her top.

"Miss, miss put your shirt back on. Miss please. I'll take the risk of having Monica find out."

As soon as those words were spoken Jeremy receives a knock on the door then someone pushes the door open slightly.

"Hey, Jeremy, the door was cracked open, so I decided to surprise you. What the hell is going on here?"

Monica shouts, as she enters Jeremy's room and notices a half-dressed Kasha standing before her.

"Oh shit, Monica, I can explain. I don't even know this woman. She just showed up in my room. I don't know why she took her shirt off. I had no intention of sleeping with her. Trust me, Monica I'd never cheat on you. I'm not that kind of guy. If you let me explain I can clear all of this up."

"Yes and I'm sure that you can. Right now, I want to speak with this whore in your room," Monica says as Kasha puts her blouse back on.

Jeremy senses the anger and tension within Monica's eyes. He quickly exits the room upon her request. He'd have to diffuse the situation later.

Monica is standing face to face with Kasha, yet again, but this time she had had enough.

"Now look, Kasha, I know sleeping with Marlin was wrong and I'm sorry for his death but I can't take back what I've done. So all of your little antics to get back at me have to end because now you're messing with me and mine and I don't allow that," Monica says.

"Oh, it's funny, how the shoe is on the other foot. Now you know how I felt when I found out my husband was screwing you. What goes around comes around. You got some nerve trying to call someone a whore. How many men have you slept with?"

"Look, Kasha, my past isn't on trial here and that's exactly what it is, my past. I've changed and I suggest you leave my man alone before I have to hurt you," Monica says walking out of the room.

"I'd like to see you try. Oh, I suggest your man pays off his gambling debt," Kasha shouts.

"What?" Monica questions her but it is too late. Kasha was already making her way down the hallway.

What was she talking about? What gambling debt? How did she know he had a gambling debt? What exactly did happen in that hotel room? Monica knew one thing was for sure, she'd definitely have to get to the bottom of all of this drama.

Chapter 23
Revealing the Truth

B ack at home, Jeremy finally explained everything that was going on. He didn't know how she would take it, but he did know that his future wife deserved the truth.

"So, what the hell happened honestly?"

"Monica, everything I said that happened really happened. I don't know that woman. I don't know how she got in my room. I never touched her. I didn't sleep with her."

"I believe you."

"Thank you."

"You're welcome. Women that are desperate make me sick. Don't let it happen again…Would you happen to know where my mother's rings are? I've been searching for them for a couple days," she says searching around the armoire in their bedroom.

"Also, Kasha said something about paying off a gambling debt. What is she talking about?"

At that moment, he knew he was busted. He'd have to confess to her the painful truth of his past gambling debts.

"Monica, I have something to tell you," he says standing in front of her.

"What is it?"

"I owe $15,000. I had a gambling problem back in college. I was trying to pay for school and things got a little out of hand. Now I have to pay this money back before the end of next week," Jeremy explains.

"What? What the hell were you gambling for?"

"To pay for college, I was going to get kicked out if I didn't pay my next semester's tuition. I owe this man. He helped me get a basketball scholarship, which in turn, landed me a spot in the pros. But now that I'm in there, I have to pay what I owe."

"Well that shouldn't be a problem, you're a freaking millionaire," Monica says excitedly.

"Uh, I have something else to tell you. After I pay the fifteen thousand from what I got in my bank account, I'll only be left with about $8500, if that."

"What the hell? Where did all of your money go? What'd you do with it? How are you paying back the fifteen grand if you're going broke, Jeremy?"

"That's the next thing I wanted to talk with you about," he says standing in front of Monica holding her hand. He hoped she wouldn't get too angry with what he was about to say.

"I hustled up some of my own money, but I was still short $500, so I took your mother's rings and had to..."

"You PAWNED my mother's rings? How could you do that? Who the fuck gave you permission to do that Jeremy? Because you needed money, you gave away items that were special to my family. I planned on giving those to Ashleigh on her prom night. How could you?" she says turning away from him.

"Monica, I'm sorry. I'll get them back."

"You didn't even ask. You just took them. You stole them, J. You stole from me. How am I supposed to marry you if I can't even trust you?"

"You *can* trust me, babe. I just need you to help me out right now until things get settled."

"Until things get settled," so is that all I am to you, a money ticket? You knew when you met me you were going broke, so you thought hooking up with a successful woman would in turn help you. All this time I thought we had something, but you were using me for my money. You want to marry me for my money."

"Monica, when I met you I didn't know anything about your career until you told me. I was attracted to you, not your status, nor your money. I love you, you know that. You know that I'm with you because I love you. I want to marry, yes, because of the money and before you get all worked up, listen to what I'm about to say. Marriage is a partnership. You help me, I help you. You help me out with a little money until I sign this endorsement deal for $2.6 million and I get back on my feet."

"I'll help you raise Ashleigh. Let's just be honest. No matter how much money you have you can't raise a child by yourself, Monica. You'll need help. You got a daughter too. Come on help me, I help you. We can make it work."

"You should've never stolen my mother's rings J."

"I told you I'd get them back.

"Let's hope so," Monica says sadly as she exits the room leaving Jeremy standing by himself.

During the next couple of days things take an interesting turn for the couple. Jeremy is trying to check all of his accounts to be sure that Mr. Isis gets all of his money and then some when the two weeks are up. But there was just one thing he didn't anticipate happening. He receives a phone call as he is shuffling through some past bank statements.

"Hello."

"Hello, may I speak with Jeremy Stuart?"

"This is he. Who am I speaking with?"

"This is Franklyn at First Federal Bank. I'm calling to let you know that we've been informed by Century 21 that the check for your condominium didn't clear. It appears you are deficient of funds."

"What do you mean I'm deficient of funds? I just paid that condominium off. I have the papers to prove it."

"Sir, our records show the check you sent for $1,900 didn't clear. So, we're going to need you to cover the amount, or the condo will become property of the bank. You have six months to take care of this discrepancy," Franklyn says.

"You'll get the money. The goddamn bank will get the fucking money!" he yells, hanging up in an angry fit.

"FUCK! FUCK! FUCK!!!" he yelled. He couldn't believe all of this was happening. It was as if it was one thing after another. What would he do? How could he pay his debt if he had another debt on top of it? He'd have to really hope this endorsement deal went through and that Monica would come through to help him out. Just when things couldn't get any worse, Jeremy gets another incoming phone call, one he wishes he'd never answered.

"Yeah, this is Jeremy."

"Jeremy, time is running out, my friend. Why haven't you paid me my money? You have only a few days left to get the $15,000 or I'll add another $500. I would hate for something to happen to your family because you couldn't pay your debt, Mr. Stuart. You get me my money by Saturday at midnight, or I'll be taking you out."

"Saturday, that's just in two days, Mr. Isis. I'll get you the money. Just don't go near my family!" he says but the phone hangs up.

"Hello! Hello! Mr. Isis, Hello! Fuck!" he says standing up and throwing his phone down on the desk. He paces around the office frantically thinking how he could come up with the rest of the money within two days if there is no money in his accounts and he owes $1,900 to the bank? Jeremy had never been in such financial turmoil like this before. How would he get out of it?

****

Meanwhile, Monica is at work bringing back some files to her office before she heads to the elevator. She and Rachel point out a handsome gentleman by the water cooler talking to some other employees. Rachel seems to be interested but doesn't want to say anything.

"Who is he?" Rachel questions enthusiastically.

"His name is Marcus King. He is my new assistant. He's been here for a few weeks now."

"He's kind of cute."

"Uh, I wouldn't go there, but if you like him, you should go talk to him," Monica suggests.

"What? Why? Normally, you're the one that's all over a man."

"But I have changed. I found the one that I need. Next time you should go talk to him. Maybe you can make me a god-mother!" Monica says, making her way over to the elevator and up to her private CEO office.

Monica places the files on her desk and feels a slight touch on her behind. She turns around and sees Marcus standing before her.

"Uh, hello, Marcus...how'd you get in here and what the hell are you doing?" Monica questions.

"I'm here to see you! I work for you, remember?" he says, moving towards Monica and running his hand down her thigh.

"Stop touching me, Marcus! I am your boss. The highest authority in this company, this is beyond inappropriate."

"Come on Monica, you know you want this. What woman could resist me?" he boasts as he touches her hand and smiles.

"Marcus, this is sexual harassment. I could have you terminated."

"Come on Monica. Don't you sleep with all of the men you work with? In fact isn't that how you got this job?" Marcus retorts.

"Excuse me, where are you getting these accusations from?"

"Don't worry yourself about how I found out; just worry what would happen if word got out about your little workplace sex-capedes."

"What are you talking about?" she questions with concern.

"Oh please, like you don't know? I know all about how you slept your way up the corporate ladder within this company. I know you slept with Mr. Perry himself."

"What the hell are you talking about?" Monica wonders.

"You might want to check that closet out and look at the top shelf. I discovered something while you had me sort out your office on your day off. It seems there were some packages sent here from your old location," Marcus says as he exits Monica's office.

Monica slams the door shut and searches for a key to open the locked cabinet. While she roams through all the piles of company invoices, she finds a box with the words, "Private" labeled on top. She opens the box to see several tapes inside. It had to be about six or seven of them. Filled with curiosity, Monica places one of the tapes into the disc player and receives the biggest shock of her life. There she was on film with Jonathan Perry. He had videotaped their sexual encounters. The more tapes she watched, the more overcome with embarrassment she became.

That's why Jonathan told her he couldn't do "this" anymore? He knew what he was doing. He was trying to save himself from getting caught and losing his job. And now that he precedes her, she may now be at risk of losing her job. What would she do if word got out? How would she be treated at work? All of her power and credibility would be gone forever with her job. What would happen if Jeremy found out? What would he think, what would he do? Would he leave her and break off their engagement?

Chapter 24
Paying Debts

A few weeks have passed since Monica found out about the secret sex videos. Things at the job have been anything but tolerable. Marcus was just making things outright uncomfortable. Monica walks into her office and sees Marcus sitting on her desk as if he was waiting on her to come in. Monica is a little uneasy, wondering what he would try this time.

"Marcus, how did you get into my office and why are you here so early?" she questions as she places her briefcase on a nearby chair. Marcus rises up and walks over to where she is standing. He places his hands around her waist backing her into a corner making it impossible to escape.

"Please, let's not start this. I told you to stop. This has been going on long enough, Marcus stop. Marcus STOP!!!!!!!" Monica pleads but he doesn't listen.

He stands back and unbuckles his pants exposing himself to Monica.

"Come on, Monica. You think you're too good for me or something?" Marcus asks as he shoves Monica across the room causing her head to hit the wall. She begins to cry out for help.

"Stop acting like such a bitch! I've been working here for three months and I'll be damn if I don't get what's mine. This is what you want, isn't it?" he rambles off angrily, as he grabs her from behind, attempting to force himself on her.

He attempts to pull down Monica's skirt while she tries to fight him off. Marcus raises his hand to slap her across the face. She quietly cries to herself.

"Stop playing hard to get. Everybody knows you're an easy lay, so stop fighting me and let me do this," Marcus threatens, but he is in for a surprise when a couple of police officers rush into the room.

One officer has a gun pointed at Marcus' head while the other is pulling him off the floor and placing him into handcuffs.

"Marcus King, you are under arrest for sexual assault," the officer says as he shoves Marcus out of the door.

"Oh, you sneaky bitch, you set me up!" Marcus yells, as he is carried out. Monica watches the cops leave her office and notices a few co-workers standing outside of the office wondering what exactly happened that landed

Marcus in handcuffs. Rachel rushes into Monica's office and shuts the door behind her. She tries to console her, but Monica just bursts into tears.

"What happened?   Monica, what's going on with Marcus?"

"Rach, for a month or so, Marcus has been trying to force himself on me!" she sobs.

"What? Oh my goodness! Why didn't you tell me? You should've said something weeks ago. I would've handled the situation. Are you alright? Did he ever..."

"No, he never went all the way with anything but he did rough me up a few times."

"Why the hell didn't you tell Jeremy?" Rachel questions.

"Because he caught me on tape..."

"On tape doing what?" Rachel wonders.

"On tape with Jonathan, he was secretly recording us having sex."

"Oh my God, I can't believe this. Does anybody know about this?"

"No one besides Marcus, I destroyed the footage. I can't believe this is happening to me. I know all of my philandering ways would catch up with me. But damn, haven't I suffered enough already?"

"Don't worry. You should just take the rest of the day off. You've been through a lot." Rachel says to Monica, as she helps her out of the room and into her car. She decides to stay with Monica to try and console her because of everything she was going through.

A Few Days Later

The heat had gotten even hotter for Jeremy with Mr. Isis. Jeremy had gone to sleep in his bed and woke up in Mr. Isis' lair with his hands tied to a chair. Mr. Isis wasn't too thrilled about Jeremy paying back his debt payments a couple of weeks later than he was supposed to. He paced around the room, never taking his eyes off Jeremy, who was shaking in fear.

"Where is my money, Jeremy?!?" Mr. Isis yells.

"I don't have it," he answers.

"Wrong answer, wrong mutherfuckin' answer asshole..." he yells smacking Jeremy across the face with the barrel of his pistol.

"I gave you two weeks, two weeks to get my money! Your two weeks are up and still no sign of my money. If you haven't learned by now, I don't play with my money. I'm sorry that I may have to do this, but if you leave me no choice. I'm going to have to take matters into my own hands," he says as he cocks the trigger of his gun and points it at Jeremy's head.

"Hey! You Mr. Isis?" a far away voice asks.

"Who is this? Come in," Mr. Isis says as he motions to his bodyguard to let the mysterious figure walk towards him with a suitcase in hand.

"Ooh, mami, who do I owe the pleasure to senorita? Who is this sexy woman?"

"I believe this is all of the money that we owe, plus interest. Now leave my man alone," Monica says dressed in a short blue dress with a pair of Manolos high hells. She figured if she was going to bail her man out of trouble she ought to look good doing it.

"How much is this?" Mr. Isis asks as he opens the suitcase to see a plethora of Benjamin Franklins neatly arranged inside.

"That is exactly $15,000 with interest so that is $2.6 million. I think that is all you need. So can you please let my man go?" she asks.

Mr. Isis takes a portion of the money out to examine it. He looks up at Jeremy who has a busted lip and a bloody nose. He unties his hands and lets Jeremy walk as a free man.

"Let's not meet again, Jeremy," Mr. Isis says as he watched Jeremy walk out of his lair.

"Thanks for bailing me out Monica. Where'd you get the money from and why'd you give him so much money?" Jeremy asks as he begins to take in the crisp night air holding a towel to his face.

"My job owed me, plus I had to make sure we never had to deal with shit like this again," Monica replies.

Monica and Jeremy are outside walking towards the car where Monica has parked several blocks down. Jeremy never would've thought that he'd be able to see the outside of Mr. Isis' lair. Things had gotten out of hand with his debt and he never knew how he'd turn things around if it wasn't for Monica's help. He was really grateful that he had met her. Now, he hoped that he could go on with the rest of his life as if none of this ever happened.

"You know, I can't thank you enough Monica, for looking out for me. I never thought I'd be a free man. I just knew for sure that Mr. Isis was going to kill me tonight."

"No problem, that's what I'm here for," Monica smiles holding on to his hand.

Monica and Jeremy is a half a block down from the car when a gunshot rang out over the streets. Monica jumps out of immediate harm and sees the most terrifying thing in her life, she knew this was serious.

"Oh, no, no Jeremy, what happened? Who did this? Oh God please don't! No! Don't leave me!" Monica cries as she realizes that Jeremy had been shot in the chest. Who could have done this? She just paid Mr. Isis, so why would he want to hurt him. Was it his way to get more revenge? Monica looked around but couldn't find a gunman until she sees a truck similar to the one that was trying to run her off the road flying around the corner.

"Karma's a bitch, bitch!" a woman yells out to Monica. She looks up to see Kasha yelling out of her car window.

Kasha shot Jeremy. Was this a way to finally get back at Monica for all the hurt she placed on her, plus taking her husband away in the process. All Monica can do is hold on to Jeremy as he struggles to catch his last breaths.

"Please, please don't leave me! I love you Jeremy, please don't leave me! Someone please call 911. Anybody, my fiancé has just been shot! Can anybody help me out?! Jeremy please don't leave me!" Monica cries as she sits in the middle of the sidewalk watching as passersby stop in their tracks. It was just one thing after another. She had just bailed him out of his debt now he gets shot anyway.

She had just gone through all of the frustration with Marcus, and let's not forget the drama of Keith and Marlin. Was all of this just a way for the world to get back at her for sleeping with so many married men? Was hurting the one man she had been waiting on her whole life her punishment? One thing was for sure, Karma is a bitch, and whatever you do comes back to you tenfold. In an instant you can lose everything that you love. Watch the dirt you put out there in the world because you never know what dirt will be sent back to you. Perhaps, that same dirt you caused will harm someone closest to you, without you even knowing it.

About the Author

Janae Marie has been writing since childhood. She began writing poetry and won several writing awards in school. Janae Marie is an American born writer/author. She was born in Detroit, MI. and has earned a college degree from Wayne State University in Media Arts & Studies. She has been writing since the age of 13. She started writing poetry as an adolescent to escape the boredom of being an only child. Filled with a mind of creativity and passion she began writing novels at the age of 16.

She has wrote several poems and has published her debut novel; Flirting with Temptations. A few stories are in the works, "Midnight Rain," The Plague," and "Leilani's Secret," for the future. She has also wrote, directed, produced and edited her very own film entitled, My Mother Donna.

"I have always wanted to be a writer to express my creativity. I am a lover of literature that also loves to entertain and inform those around me. My mission as a writer is to entertain, educate and inform young adults that are interested in the literary world."

Flirting with Temptations is the first book by new author Janae Marie

Soon to come from Janae Marie: *"Midnight Rain,"* *"Leilani's Secret,"* and *"The Plague."*

www.ingramcontent.com/pod-product-compliance
Lightning Source LLC
Chambersburg PA
CBHW070928130626
46555CB00001B/332